RETURN OF THE LIVING

ELVES

Bryan!

Merry fuckin' Xmes!

BRIAN

A MUTATED MEDIA PRODUCTION

Edited by Mort Stone and Candace Nola

Cover Art by Marc Vuletich

Interior Layout by Lori Michelle
www.TheAuthorsAlley.com

Also by Brian Asman

I'm Not Even Supposed to be Here Today
(Eraserhead Press)
Jailbroke
Nunchuck City
Man, Fuck This House

Coming Soon

Our Black Hearts Beat as One

Also by Shelly Lyons

Like Real

PRAISE FOR
RETURN OF THE LIVING ELVES

"It's hard not to admire the gonzo ambition of this cheeky holiday fright fest . . . an entertaining hodgepodge of Christmas and zombie fiction tropes."

—*Kirkus Reviews*

"This Yuletide-themed homage to one of the greatest zombie films ever made is a rollicking good time. Brian Asman delivers laughs and gory thrills galore in a book sure to put you in the holiday spirit—if you don't get disemboweled first. Eat the fruitcake and take the ride."

—Bryan Smith, author of *68 Kill*

"With *Return of the Living Elves*, Brian Asman shows he's the funniest, goriest, scariest comedy-horror creator this side of James Gunn. If you loved *Man, Fuck This House* (and you should love *Man, Fuck This House*), you're going to absolutely flip for this one."

—Nick Kolakowski,
author of *Absolute Unit* and *Love & Bullets*

"Funny, action-packed, and killer Elves . . . a Christmas gift that keeps on giving."

—HorrorDNA

"Brian Asman's *Return of the Living Elves* is a wild, sleigh ride whiplash of quips, gore, and heartfelt humor. It belongs on every bookshelf, right between Romero and Dickens. I loved it!"

—Shawn Mansouri, author of *Spare Parts*

Twas the night before Christmas,
And all through Pine Canyon
Brian Asman was shamelessly
Ripping off Dan O'Bannon.
He boldly declared,
With Grinch-greedy eyes,
"The Return of the Living Dead,
I shall Christmatize!"
He stole dialogue and plot points
With no hint of remorse,
Copied characters aplenty
Took motivations by force!
He swore and he sweated
And giggled to himself,
When he shoehorned in a joke
About Elf on the Shelf,
On groaners! On cliches! On purplish prose!
(How'd he get that MFA? Blackmail, I suppose)
He gleefully trod o'er the line,
Betwixt theft and homage,
Spewing six-dollar words,
Like obdurate and decolletage.
Churching up a classic movie
About zombies and punks,
Hot blondes named Trash,
And leathered, mohawked lunks.
Loading up his MS
With in-jokes and puns,
Mistaking 'member-berries references
For smart Yuletide fun.
"Haha! There's a warehouse
With two working stiffs,
A gaggle of youngsters,

And a corpse in the mix!
Except it's not our dear Tarman
Long-suspended in sludge
But a bloodthirsty elf
Who gives not a fudge?!"
It's a tribute, a paean
To good will and good cheer
With copious helpings
Of intestines and fear,
It's a Xerox, for sure,
Unoriginal dreck,
But with a Brian Asman book
What the fuck did you expect?
Just pop culture references
Mutant monsters and tits,
If you want fuckin' Shakespeare
Go read *As You Like It*
Now sit back, relax, with a tall glass of milk
Oven-fresh cookies, pajamas of silk
Get comfy, get ready, for a riveting tale,
Or a half-baked cash-grab flying fast off the rails.
Either way if you're holding this book in your hands,
Just remember this mantra,
scream it across the land,
Whether poor and downtrodden,
Or lousy with riches
You bought this motherfucker,
NO REFUNDS, BITCHES.

December 24th, 2019
5:30pm Pacific Standard Time
Whosgotta Christmas Supply Warehouse
Pine Canyon, CA

THE KID DIDN'T look like much, but then again Jimmy Ricci'd seen enough in his nigh-thirty years working the nightshift at Whosgotta Christmas Supply Warehouse to know appearances could be deceiving.

Then AGAIN again, he'd never had a new recruit show up for work in goddamn CLOWN PAINT before.

"Grab a seat," Jimmy said, motioning to the chair on the other side of his desk. The kid stepped into the office, skittish like a baby deer who'd just been offered a salt lick by a pervert in an off-white panel van. He tried to sit down, but the proffered chair was covered with yellowing invoices, like every other surface in the cramped, smoky, windowless office.

"What should I—"

"Just put 'em on the floor," Jimmy grunted, eyes flicking back to the application in his hand.

Tom Sadler. Nineteen years old. Five-ten, one-sixty. Recent graduate of Russo High. Did a nickel at Angelo's Pizza. Busboy, line cook. Worked his way up to cashier, then—

"Why'd you leave Angelo's?"

The kid shrugged. "My girlfriend said I wasn't going nowhere. I should, you know, branch out."

"And you think humping candy canes and

1

nutcrackers from one end of the warehouse to the other's what moving up in the world looks like?"

"I dunno."

Jimmy put the application down on a hefty stack of dead trees—his own might've been buried in there, somewhere. They never threw nothing away at Whosgotta.

"What do you know, kid?"

Clownface picked at a scab on his elbow.

"Okay, tell me this. Why us? Why not, I dunno, Starbucks? They pay decent wages, and some of those kids got tattoos on their faces. That's like permanent clown paint."

The kid looked up, something serious forcing its way through the greasepaint. "I don't want to work nowhere CORPORATE. It's against my e-thos."

"The fuck's an e-thos?"

"You know, like my beliefs."

Jimmy leaned back in his swivel chair, both hairy hands resting on his ample stomach—the Double Barreled MeatBlast from Angelo's had gotten him through more than one lonely night at the warehouse. "You mean your beliefs, or LIKE your beliefs?"

"Huh?"

Jimmy shook his head, the swivel chair groaning. "Never mind, kid." He narrowed his eyes at the newcomer. "One last question—what's with the face paint?"

"Face paint?"

"Yeah, you flunk outta Clown College on account of being deaf?"

The kid looked like Jimmy just asked him an algebra question, the square root of a hundred or something. He mumbled, "I'm a Juggalo."

"You bang old broads for money? Good for you, kid, although I don't see how the clown stuff fits in."

"No, a JUGG-A-LO. Insane Clown Posse? Whoop whoop?"

Jimmy scanned the application again. "Says here you speak English?"

"Yeah?"

"Start doing that." Jimmy stood, chair springs squeaking a sigh of relief. "You ready to get started?"

The kid blinked. "You mean I got the job?"

"Yeah, now hurry up and shake my damn hand before I give it to the next clown who comes through the door."

The kid popped out of his chair, grabbed Jimmy's paw, furiously pumping his arm.

Nice, firm handshake—Jimmy liked that. Most of the namby-pamby, stick-armed little twerps his age, they didn't know how to shake hands no more. Somebody'd raised this kid right.

Jimmy clapped the kid on the shoulder, steering him towards the office door. "Gonna give you the grand tour, then we'll get started. Ordinarily night shift doesn't start till eight, but tonight's the big show."

"The big show?"

"That's right, kid. Christmas Eve. The second the stores close, they break down all their holiday junk and ship it right back here."

"To us?"

"Exactly. Window displays, novelty presents, that big old throne they sit Kris Kringle on? The second the stores can get rid of that crap, they do. We inventory it, check for damages—invoice 'em, of course—and put it all away for another year."

The kid gaped at him. "Wow!"

Wasn't so *wow* for Jimmy anymore, but even though he'd been doing this for thirty years, he never forgot why he got into it in the first place.

In Jimmy's mind, Christmas really was the most wonderful time of the year, and he got to drink it in 24/7.

Through a goddamn firehose, sometimes, but STILL.

"Follow me, kid, time's a-wasting." Jimmy barreled onto the warehouse floor, a cavernous space the size of a football field lined with rows of metal shelving. Half of them empty, the rest sagging under the weight of unwanted crates of Christmas merchandise.

He pointed to the rollup doors at the far end. "Down there's the loading dock, where we stage all the returns. Gonna take us weeks to put all this shit away, so your job's secure until then. Ha!"

"Just a couple weeks?"

Jimmy grinned. "Don't worry, kid, you do a good job, we'll keep you on year-round."

"What's there to do for the rest of the year?"

Jimmy led him down an aisle filled with plastic snowmen. "The perverts keep us in business." He grabbed a snowman with an uncomfortably-large carrot nose off the rack. "See old Frosty here? Come February, when they're jonesing, those creeps'll pay top dollar for sturdy, dependable craftsmanship." Jimmy smacked the snowman on the side of the head. Cracks spider-webbed out from the impact. "Must be defective. Anyway, I'm not gonna judge another man for how he gets his holly-jollies, no sir. I'll show you where the rejects go later." He tossed the snowman on the ground.

"Way it's organized," Jimmy continued, "you've got your humanoid characters on these rows, then livestock, camels and such, manger scenes, inflatables, novelty presents—you know, those big cardboard things you always see at department stores—and finally trees. Lots and lots of fake trees." Jimmy pointed to a small, handwritten sign affixed to the end of the aisle. "See here? This aisle, that's the SMLs, SMMs, and SMSs. You wanna take a guess what an SML is?"

The kid's mouth moved slowly. No sound came out.

Jimmy gave him a paternal smile. "That's okay, took me a few years to get it down pat. Check this out." He pointed a plump finger at the *S.* "The *S*, see, that stands for *Snow*. And the *M,* that's *Man. L's Large.* Snow. Man. Large."

The kid nodded. "Makes sense."

"Learning already. I like it. Now, how about the SMMs?"

"Snowman . . . " the kid stared off into the distance, as if the answer could be found amongst the spider-filled rafters. "Mentos?"

"Don't get fresh with me, kid." Jimmy laughed at his own joke. "Nope, that second *M,* it stands for medium. And so, the SMSs—"

"Snowman Small!"

"Now you're cooking with grease. Let me throw you a real brain teaser. The SMLs, for example, are divided up into SMLCCs and SMLPs. I'll give you a hint." Jimmy pointed at a huge snowman with a pipe stuck between its teeth. "This here's an SMLCC. You probably think that CC stands for Courtney Cox, seeing how there's more than a passing resemblance, but no, it stands for—"

"Corn cob!"

Jimmy ruffled the kid's hair. "Careful. Roberta hears you talking like that on your first day, she might just make you manager."

The kid beamed. "Really?"

"Running me out of a job already. Saints preserve us. Now come on, we got a lot of ground to cover before the trucks start rolling in."

Jimmy gave him the five-cent tour, pointing out the mistletoe, wreaths, reindeer—Rudolph had his own section, of course—then took him back to the office. "Now, the most important part. How to clock in. Here's your time card."

The kid took it reverently, like the Holy Bible itself, or at least a Chick tract.

"Stick it in the machine, right there."

The kid looked at the time clock like a monkey who'd found a crashed satellite in his favorite banana patch. Poked it with a finger, then—miraculously—stuck the card in the right way.

PUNCH!

"What time did you say I get off again?"

Jimmy made a show of glancing at his Timex, favored the kid with his best Serious Boss™ look. "Tonight? We'll have to see how it goes, but I can probably let you outta here by four."

"AM?"

"That's the one."

The kid's face fell, or as much as it could underneath all the goddamn clown paint. "All night?"

"What's the matter, kid? Afraid of a little hard work?"

"Not that. It's just—" the kid trailed off, looking at his shoes—Converse All-Stars instead of size 13 floppers, which made very little sense to Jimmy.

"Come on, kid, out with it."

"The stores'll be closed by then."

"Well yeah, it's Christmas."

"I'm screwed." The kid sat down heavily, hung his head.

Jimmy dropped to his haunches. "Whatever it is, you can tell Uncle Jimmy."

"I been so busy, looking for a new job and everything, I, uh, forgot to get my girlfriend a Christmas present."

"That's no good. I hear women are partial to those."

The kid nodded. "Remembered on the way over here. Oh man, I'm dead!" He buried his face in his hands.

Jimmy hadn't had anyone to buy Christmas presents for in a good long while, not since Lorna left—*have fun with your reindeer games, asshole*—but he could sympathize. And it WAS Christmas, or Christmas Eve at least.

And there had to be some unwritten rule, if a guy with a belly like his had the opportunity to summon up a Christmas miracle from the bowels of the Whosgotta Christmas Supply Warehouse?

He was HONOR BOUND, damn it.

Jimmy yanked the kid up by his elbow. "Can the waterworks, Ronald. I got just the thing for you."

The kid looked up at him, beaming with hope. "Really?

Jimmy grinned, spreading his arms wide. "Just call me St. Nick."

6:04pm Pacific Standard Time

"Step lively, kid," Jimmy said, reaching the bottom of the stairs. Mildew hung in the air, water drip-drip-dripped from a rusty pipe somewhere. He fumbled around for the light switch, hand brushing what he hoped was fake snow—he did NOT need a repeat of the infamous Brown Recluse Bite of '84.

CLICK.

The overheads came on, illuminating the basement—a cramped, dingy space considerably smaller than the warehouse upstairs, crammed with all the bullshit they had no use for but couldn't throw away. Mostly special-order Christmas decorations.

Like the nativity scene some dentist ordered—toothbrushes dressed up as Mary and Joseph, a plastic incisor the size of a bowling ball standing in for little baby Jesus.

Or the leather daddy Santa and his nine gimpy reindeer, complete with ball gags for bridles.

Or the tiny penis-shaped Christmas lights, a cast-off from what Jimmy surmised had to be the bachelorette party from Hell.

Then again, maybe those went with the nine gimpy reindeer, who the fuck knew?

"Wow," the kid said, voice thick with genuine awe. "This is the coolest."

"Like I said, Christmas attracts all kinds. This way." Jimmy weaved through assorted stacks of junk, dodging pools of shadow he assumed to be lousy with spiders, making his way to the back. "Now, we've got a firm *no returns* policy on custom jobs, not like the standard stuff the department stores rent every year. Problem is, this crap has a way of showing up on our doorstep anyway." He shoved a plastic Santa painted up to look like Donald Trump, which knocked over another Santa done up like Barack Obama, which dominoed yet another Santa in Dubya's likeness, on and on until a red-suited George Washington lay face down in a puddle of something foul.

Jimmy raised an eyebrow. "Soon as we're done upstairs, you're picking all this shit up."

"Yeah, okay," the kid said.

They reached the back of the basement, where a padlocked door waited. Jimmy held up a key—must've been a hundred on his ring—and waggled his eyebrows. "Not all the returns are crap. There's some real treasures in here. And like I said, I got just the thing for your lady friend."

"Boy, I hope so!"

Jimmy unlocked the door, flung it wide. The faint scents of pine and peppermint wafted out.

"Always smells good, this room," Jimmy said. "No idea why. Rest of the basement's like a skunk took a shit in a septic tank. Anyway—" He flipped on the light.

The room was small. A couple metal shelves held various knickknacks, but the main attraction was a big wooden crate.

"What's in there?" the kid asked.

"Trade secret." Jimmy grabbed a crowbar, went to work. The crate cracked when he pried the lid up, rusty nails sticking out like twisted teeth. "Go on, have a look."

The kid approached the crate cautiously.

"Watch out for splinters," Jimmy said.

The kid peered inside the crate. His eyes went wide.

Jimmy leaned back against the wall, tapping the crowbar against the heel of his boot. *Now THAT'S a Christmas miracle, you magnificent son of a bitch.*

"You've gotta be kidding!" The kid whirled, holding up a snow globe. But not just any snow globe, no sirree. The base was filigreed silver, the dome filled with swirling flecks of white gold, creating such a maelstrom it was impossible to see the diorama within. But who the fuck cared about THAT?

Jimmy took a peek inside the crate himself. There, on top of one of the other snow globes, was a fruitcake, Saran wrapped, and looking semi-appetizing for something that'd been confined to the basement for who knew how many years. Jimmy's mouth watered at the sight, but he left it alone. He had a strict policy about eating foodstuffs found in the warehouse—only in the most dire of emergencies.

The kid danced around the room, practically pirouetting, globe held high. "This is beautiful! Landfill's gonna love it."

Jimmy blinked. "Landfill?"

The kid paused, holding the snow globe tightly to his chest. "That's my girlfriend."

"And her name's—"

"Landfill."

"She a juggler, too?"

"More of a Christpunk. She likes Blaze Ya Dead Homie though."

Jimmy sighed. "Kid, I have no idea what the hell any of that means, but as long as she's happy, you know?"

The kid bobbed his head animatedly, heading for the door. "Oh, she's gonna lo—"

He tripped over his own feet.

The snow globe sailed end-over-end, slo-mo, like a football replay.

Hit the ground.

Shattered.

Jimmy heard somebody yell "No!" and figured it was probably him.

Then the room filled with snow and the lights went out.

6:17pm Pacific Standard Time

Miles away, a motley crew of wayward youth meandered down the street, sipping hot chocolate in paper bags and looking for a corner free of *No Loitering* signs.

"Where we gonna go Christmas caroling?" the skinny boy they called Caterpillar asked.

The youth next to him, a blonde Christpunk named Landfill, who just so happened to be the girlfriend of the Juggalo who was currently choking to death on mysterious artificial snow in the bowels of the Whosgotta Christmas Supply Warehouse, spat on the sidewalk and said, "How about Atheist Acres?"

"They said they'd shoot us if we went back there," the tallest and beefiest one, Self-Harm, said. He wore a leather jacket covered in Bible verses and had "Hova" tattooed in blue ink across his forehead—a body art decision that often caused people to confuse him for a fan of Jay-Z's utterly godless "music" instead of a devotee of the almighty Yahweh.

"No way I'm going there," Caterpillar said. "I heard it's bad luck to die on Christmas Eve."

"It's bad luck to die any day."

Caterpillar scowled. "Yeah, but especially on Christmas. You think Jesus wants to deal with your shit on his birthday? Hell no, man. He's busy blowing out like ten billion birthday candles, he ain't got time for that."

Self-Harm cracked his knuckles. "Six THOUSAND candles. You better watch it, you're sounding like those fucking atheists."

"Cut it out, both of ya," Landfill growled. "Seriously, where we gonna go?"

The three Christpunks hung their heads in silence, despairing of ever finding the right street to fill with their joyful noises.

"Hey, what about Tom?" Caterpillar said.

"That Juggalo?" Self-Harm scoffed.

"He ALWAYS knows the best places to go caroling."

Landfill shook her head. "He got that new job. You know, at the Christmas place?"

"He selling Christmas trees?" Caterpillar asked. "Because dude's gonna come home covered in sap, get cat hair stuck all over him. End up looking like a Bigfoot, then somebody gonna shoot him. Turn his corpse in for the re-ward, but then they gonna DNA test him and that shit's gonna come back negative, and then old Tommy Boy, he died for NOTHING."

"It's a warehouse," Landfill said, rolling her eyes.

"Why don't we just go over there and wait till he's on break?" Self-Harm said. "They get breaks, right?"

Caterpillar swigged his hot chocolate. "How would I know? I look like a Christmas tree salesman to you? All covered in sap and cat hair, getting shot at by dumbass hunters think I'm a Sasquatch?"

"He doesn't SELL Christmas trees. They've got decorations."

"Screw this, let's go." Self-Harm tossed the remains of his hot chocolate in the recycling like a good boy and crossed the street to where he'd parked his golf cart—"I bother" spray painted on the side. He pounded the steering wheel. "Youse two coming or not?"

Landfill hopped in the back, while Caterpillar jumped in the passenger seat, mumbling something about being allergic to sap.

Self-Harm fired up the golf cart. "And a one, and a two—"

In perfect unison, the three Christpunks broke into song:

> "Here we come a-wassailing
> Among the leaves so green;
> Here we come a-wand'ring
> So fair to be seen.

Love and joy come to you
'Cause we'll wassail till we spew
MOTHERFUCKAZ."

6:31pm Pacific Standard Time

Jimmy blinked.

As a [late] middle-aged American male, he'd been blinking for years, thought he'd gotten pretty good at it. Not so. Now his eyelashes stuck together like a Sears catalog—the power tools section, on account of his greasy hands. He wasn't no pervert like the damn Santa-strokers who kept them in business during the off-season.

He grumbled, wiped his eyes with the hem of his shirt.

Somewhere behind him, the kid moaned.

He tried to remember what had happened. The snow globe broke—the kid never mentioned he had oven mitts for hands on his resume—musta been filled with some kind of poison. Jimmy rolled over, hacked up a lung. Finally forced his eyes open.

"Oh, so you ARE alive," a high-pitched voice squeaked.

Jimmy screamed, popping up to his feet like a much younger and lighter man. "Who's there?"

A slight jingle came from the shadows and a tiny figure stepped out.

Two feet tall, neon green skin. Half of its face missing, skin hanging loose and ragged over yellowing bone.

And, oh yeah.

Wearing an elf outfit.

"You gotta be shitting me," Jimmy mumbled.

"Holy bananas," the kid said, suddenly at Jimmy's elbow, wiping dust and clown paint away from his eyes. Leaving him looking like a bozo who'd been out in the sun too long.

The—there really was no other word for it, ELF— looked them up and down. "I actually thought you were dead. Didn't look like you were breathing, and the smell—"

"Hey, I shower sometimes," Jimmy said.

"You're not my first choices, but you'll do." The elf stroked his chin menacingly. Green skin flaked off, swirling like putrid snowflakes before settling on the storage room floor.

The kid looked at Jimmy. "What's he mean? Also, why's he an elf?"

"Good questions," Jimmy said. "Hey guy, this warehouse is for DECORATIONS ONLY. No real elves, you hear me?" Maybe it was the gas, or maybe he'd conked his noggin but good, because all of a sudden Jimmy couldn't understand a goddamn word that was coming out of his own mouth.

The elf smiled, displaying several rows of pointy teeth—at least four. Rows, not teeth.

Jimmy's balls sucked up into his abdomen.

"My name," the elf said, "is Elfphonso. But you can call me GOD." He hissed and ran at Jimmy.

Without thinking, Jimmy grabbed the crowbar off the floor and swung with all his might. The crowbar crashed into the elf's skull, sent him pin wheeling out the doorway.

"Get the door, kid!" Jimmy bellowed.

The kid lunged for the door. The elf popped his head back in, teeth gleaming. The kid kicked the elf away, then slammed the door shut.

"Let me in!" Elfphonso screamed through the door, banging on the frame. "Don't deny your destiny, you fools!"

Jimmy shot the kid a look. "Way to go, butter fingers."

"Open the door and join me! I will make you powerful beyond measure."

"Not my fault," the kid muttered. "You're the one who gave me a cursed globe."

"It's not CURSED," Elfphonso's muffled voice explained. "The globe was merely—"

Jimmy threw himself against the door. "I got this. Drag that crate over here, kid."

The kid nodded and pulled on the crate. It didn't move.

"Try pushing, kid," Jimmy said. "And use your legs. I can't afford no workman's comp."

The kid circled around the crate, tried pushing. It moved an inch, maybe two.

"Come on, kid, put your back into it!"

Pressing his back into the crate and jamming his Converse tennies against the floor, the kid grunted, strained with all his might.

Slowly, a centimeter at a time, the crate inched across the floor.

"What are you doing?" Elfphonso called. "That sounds heavy."

The door thumped against Jimmy's weight.

"Might want to turn on the afterburners, kid. Dunno how much longer this thing's gonna hold."

"Whoop . . . whoop!" the kid shouted, then gave

the crate one last heave-ho. Jimmy jumped out of the way just as the crate slammed into the door.

"Good work, kid," Jimmy said, clapping him on the shoulder. "Now, let's take some of this other junk and make a real Maginot line."

"Didn't the Germans run right over that?"

Jimmy scowled. "We make it through the next ten minutes, you can give me all the history lessons you want. Now!"

Jimmy and the kid grabbed boxes, smaller crates, whatever they could get their hands on, stacking anything that didn't have a pulse in front of the door. On the other side, the creature from the snow globe alternately threatened, begged, and got weirdly depressive, talking about maybe just sticking his head in the oven if he couldn't find one single person to join his undead elf army to overthrow the Clausian Hegemony or some such nonsense; Jimmy wasn't even paying attention. The elf's bullshit just became one buzzing, droning noise, like an air conditioner or his ex-wife, Lorna.

"At least give me the crate," the elf pleaded. "I need it. For a school project."

"Get the fuck out of my warehouse!" Jimmy bellowed.

"Fine, but I'll be back," the elf hissed. "With an army!"

"Yeah, yeah," Jimmy replied, rearranging their improvised barricade for maximum keep-elves-outtitude. "You do you, short stack."

The elf said something Jimmy found particularly unkind, given the circumstances, and then Jimmy heard the tiny pitter-patter of undead elf feet fading away across the basement.

Barricade built, Jimmy and the kid collapsed on either side of the junk pile.

Jimmy wondered if the elf was really gone, or if he was up to something. Looking for an air vent? Trying to find a way in?

There weren't any ducts in the room, so that was good.

Or maybe it wasn't. Just how much air was in the little storage room, anyway?

"Uh, Jimmy?"

Jimmy mopped his sweaty brow with the hem of his shirt. "What is it, kid?"

"I, uh, I don't feel so good."

"Me either. Getting attacked by a zombie elf'll do that to ya."

"No, that's not—here, look."

Jimmy turned to the kid, who was holding out his ankle. A pretty nasty-looking wound peeped through a ragged tear in his jeans, blood soaked into his socks.

Even through all the clown paint, the kid's face looked horribly pale.

"I think he got me, Jimmy."

Jimmy swallowed, big time. "I think you're right, kid."

Shit.

9:34pm Arctic Time

Most nights, he dreamed of Lollipopland.

And woke up screaming.

RETURN OF THE LIVING ELVES

The dreams started innocuously enough—him and the rest of his Krampus Corps unit dropping out of a stealth sleigh at 30,000 feet, oxygen masks tight over their faces. Hurtling through the night, the sugar-sprinkled landscape getting closer and closer—

Landing in a sea of chocolate, the melting cocoa sticking to his dungarees. Cutting off his parachute with his combat knife, his brother corpsmen rising from the black muck with KK-47s at the ready.

Then the machine gun nests on the beach roared to life and blew them all to hell.

Nobody knew the Lollipoplanders had heavy ordnance. Or somebody knew and didn't bother telling him. He figured even odds either way.

One thing he'd learned from a lifetime of swallowing reindeer shit in this man's army?

NEVER trust a Claus.

When the shooting was over, only one other corpsman was still breathing. They swam north, drug their asses out of the ocean, sticky with both chocolate and the blood of their brothers. Hid in the Licorice Forest, hunted gummy rabbits to survive.

God, the way they giggled when he cut them open—

Weeks later, a couple of Pieanese rebels—they'd harbored a grudge ever since Colonel Quataffy violently annexed their homeland of Pieanmar—found him. By then he was alone, the other Corpsman having been crushed to death by a knot of falling rock candy. The head of the rebels, a stale old boysenberry with filling seeping from the slits in his round face, called in a helicopter to extract him. One excruciating debrief later, and he was asleep in his own bed.

Or trying to.

Because his body might have made it home, but his mind? His soul?

Screaming in fudge-black darkness for all etern—

BRAMMMP! BRAMMMP! BRAMMMP!

Private Matt Kringle started awake, knocking his coffee off the desk with a boot.

"Shit," he snarled, looking for a rag, a towel, something, while the sirens droned on and the bright red bulbs in the hulking supercomputer flashed, and his lukewarm coffee bled into the carpet.

At least his coffee cup hadn't shattered—*World's Best C.O.*, it said, a gift from the boys on the night he made Master Sergeant. Those boys were long dead now, and he'd lost his rank in the same fiasco, busted all the way back down to Private and stuck with the shittiest detail the North Pole had to offer.

But at least he still had the coffee mug.

Kringle tossed a handful of napkins on the spreading stain and turned to the console. He didn't know what half the buttons did, since they were strictly Need to Know and nobody told him shit, but he did know how to tell the goddamn sirens to shut the fuck up. Did they really need to be that loud? Especially inside a tiny Quonset hut, where the noise just ping-ponged off the metal walls, shredding his ear drums?

He hit a couple of buttons that looked promising, and the noise cut off, thankfully. The red lights stopped flashing, too, and maybe he'd get really lucky and not end up with a Christmas migraine after all.

Then he checked the display, saw what had

triggered the alarm, and figured a debilitating headache was the least of his worries.

He grabbed the phone, pressed the only button once, and waited for his call to connect.

"Merry Christmas," a dull, bored voice said.

"Merry Christmas," Kringle replied perfunctorily. "I'm out in Stocking 43-D, just got an alert. Some place down south called Pine Canyon."

"Probably a false alarm."

Kringle rubbed the soggy napkins on the floor with the toe of his boot, working the stain as best he could. "Yeah, I know, but procedure, right? Who's up?"

"Colonel Claus, Rancho Navidad."

All the Colonels were named Claus. Got pretty confusing, especially when one of the Generals—also all named Claus—wanted to pin the blame on somebody for their latest ill-advised bout of military adventurism. So, they usually appended whatever fancy, gated development the higher-ranking officer lived in, so they'd all know who the fuck they were talking about.

"Great, Rancho Navidad." Kringle cursed his shitty luck. Of course, it had to be her.

That spooky fucking she-devil.

"Patch me through?" Kringle asked, yanking out the desk drawer, pushing file folders aside, hoping none of the other grunts stole his emergency bottle of sugarplum schnapps.

The call connected just as his fingers brushed metal at the bottom of the drawer, no bottle to be found.

7:01pm Pacific Standard Time

Clyde "Clue" Francis steered his big rig with one hand and scratched his balls with the other, idly listening to a true crime podcast on the stereo. Reason why the other truckers called him Clue, he was obsessed with the stuff. TOO obsessed, according to Donna the Dispatcher, who liked to joke that he was just taking lessons. She got under Clue's skin but good, yet at the same time everybody knew he was a gentle giant who wasn't ACTUALLY taking correspondence courses in how to get away with slaughtering lot lizards willy-nilly.

The boy sure loved him some true crime, though. Right then he was learning all about the Trinity murders, a grotesque robbery-gone-wrong that rocked Louisville back in the '80s. The narrator had just gotten to the part where the killers and victims crossed paths at a Moby Dick restaurant.

"Moby Dick," Clue muttered, nodding along. For his part, he couldn't figure out why anybody would name their joint after a whale. ESPECIALLY a fictional one. But like his grand-mammy used to say, "It takes all kinds, you retarded piece of shit."

Clue lowered the volume a hair and pulled into the parking lot of Whosgotta. The place looked deserted. He hoped they were ready for him, because he was pissed off about having to work on Christmas in the first place. Usually he had the night off, went down to the local homeless shelter, ladled out soup and what-not. Being a trucker, he'd never had much luck keeping a family at home, so he liked to find family wherever he could.

He slowed, turned his rig in a long, yawning half-circle, and then backed up to the loading dock. Frowned in the rearview—the damn roll-up door was still closed. Now he'd have to get out and go bang on the door until somebody opened up. Easily adding a very unnecessary ten minutes onto his day.

"Be right back," Clue said, shutting off his tape deck. He swung the door open, hefted himself down to the asphalt. Pain lanced from the bottoms of his feet up through his knees.

Every time he got out of his rig, he swore he'd never go to a Sonic again, and every time he passed one on the road, he broke that vow without a second thought.

Clue lumbered around to the loading dock. Tried the regular-sized door next to the roll-up.

No dice.

"Hey, anybody home?" He rapped on the door with the backs of his knuckles.

The quiet started feeling a tad bit personal.

He was about to hop back in the rig, take all the department store junk right back to Venturini's and tell that pencil-necked assistant manager geek to deal with it himself, when he heard a sound.

Metal scraping against metal.

Sweeter than all the Hallelujah choruses put together.

Slowly, the roll-up door opened, inch by inch.

Clue crossed to the loading dock. "Hey, I was starting to think you guys were out. Got a delivery from—" He stopped talking when he realized nobody was there. He stuck his neck inside the warehouse. "Uh, hello?"

"My, aren't you a big boy. Major Santa vibes."

Clue looked around, still didn't see anyone. "It's Christmas Eve, you don't have to be all nasty to me."

"Trust me," the voice said, "It's a compliment."

Then four rows of sharp, needle-like teeth sunk into his calf and Clue screamed in pain.

He died hoping maybe someday, somebody would do a podcast about him.

7:13pm Pacific Standard Time

Jimmy stood over the kid's body, chest heaving, bloody crowbar dangling from his hand.

"Damn it."

The last few minutes seemed like a bad dream, the kind of thing one would find in a low-budget horror flick, not a semi-classy Christmas warehouse. Logically, he could follow everything that happened, A to B to C, easy peasy.

The kid had dropped an old snow globe, somehow releasing a zombie elf, who'd bitten the kid on the ankle, who then sweated and writhed and foamed at the mouth, eyes eventually rolling back in his head. He shuddered, and died, then rose again, possessed of a few more rows of teeth than when he'd shuffled off this mortal coil, and a very predictable hunger for human flesh.

"I had no choice," Jimmy said softly to himself,

trying not to look at the kid's bashed-in skull, the fragments of blood and brain speckling the walls. "I had no choice, okay?"

His voice echoed off the storage room walls, and a part of him pretended the heady resound was an answer, a confirmation. Something he could tuck in the hollows of his heart and carry with him for the rest of his life.

However long that was.

The room swayed. Jimmy swayed with it, darkness tainting the edges of his vision. He felt light-headed. Blood sugar—he'd been diagnosed with diabetes just a few years before, which was honestly less of a surprise than a foregone conclusion, considering his genetics and his weight and his lifestyle.

Not to mention his luck—mediocre at best.

Jimmy needed to eat something. He had some candy bars in his desk, but that was all the way upstairs, and there was an elf on the loose. At some point he'd probably have to go see what was going on, maybe call the police—MAYBE, because how the hell was he going to explain a bloody crowbar and a dead kid in clown makeup? He sounded stupid just THINKING about his possible excuses. They'd haul him away for sure, and he'd be damn lucky to end up in the looney bin instead of the gas chamber.

Nah, no police. Not yet. At least not until he got his blood sugar up and could fucking THINK.

Think Think THINK!

He searched the kid's pockets, hoping for some candy, a fucking Mentos, anything, but all he found was lint, a small bag of shitty weed, and a bunch of folded-up notebook paper with nonsense scrawled on it that Jimmy eventually figured to be songs.

Jimmy looked from the absolutely terrible, derivative lyrics about clowns killing rednecks to the kid's body and back again. "Maybe dead is better, kid," he said sadly, the best benediction Tom Sadler would ever receive, as his doting mother would later be killed in a bizarre incident at the local mall and his father was five years in Arizona, playing coke and doing golf, or the other way around, even Don Sadler himself wasn't sure anymore.

Energy leached from Jimmy's body. Every movement became a chore, every thought a Herculean effort that seemed less and less worth it. He needed some—

Fruitcake!

Sure, maybe it came in a crate with a bunch of snow globes that had zombie elves imprisoned in them—probably, maybe the other snow globes had cyborg unicorns or incredibly horny Bigfeet, Jimmy sure as fuck wasn't going to open them and find out— but it was fruitcake. All the sugar he needed, and fruitcake didn't go BAD, did it?

Nah. Maybe he'd get a little drunk off the fermenting fruit, but it wouldn't kill him.

Probably.

Then again, lapsing into a diabetic coma at the feet of a teenaged clown corpse would probably be even WORSE for his health.

Jimmy carefully pushed snow globes aside until he found the fruitcake, still neatly imprisoned in Saran wrap. He worked a corner free with his nail. Swooned. Ripped the rest of the plastic off, brought it to his mouth, and took a HUGE bite.

Swallowed without tasting. Took another—actually

tasted good, better than most of the fruitcake he'd ever had, the consolation prize of all holiday treats.

Within seconds, the fruitcake was gone. Jimmy felt better. MUCH better. The lightheadedness abated, and in fact, he felt energized. Adrenaline coursed through his veins. He could do this! Climb mountains, part seas, and figure out what to do with the dead body in his storage room.

Oh yeah, AND track down that little elfy SOB and put a human-sized boot up his two-foot-tall tucchus.

"It's on, you son of a bitch!" Jimmy yelled at the ceiling. "You ho-ho-hear me?"

Jimmy clamped a hand over his mouth, like he was stifling a burp in particularly appealing mixed company.

Weird.

Jimmy picked up the crowbar, brandished it menacingly, and tried again. "You hear me? I'm gonna beat your ho-ho-ho-head in!"

The crowbar clattered to the pavement. Jimmy froze, trying to figure out how he'd acquired such a bizarre verbal tic in such a short amount of time. Maybe it was trauma; braining your newest hire couldn't be great for your mental health. Or maybe he'd inhaled something—asbestos, these old Christmas decorations were full of the stuff—and now he was hallucinating.

At that point, Jimmy would've welcomed madness.

Especially when his face started itching something fierce. He brushed a cheek, felt several days' worth of stubble.

Even though he'd shaved his face baby-butt smooth that very morning.

POP!

Something pinged off the far wall. Jimmy braced himself for another elf attack, then realized he'd burst a button on his trousers. His already ample stomach was straining against his size 42 Haggar's.

"What the ho is going on?" Jimmy muttered, wondering what you might call the polar opposite of a Christmas miracle.

10:45pm Arctic Time

Private Matt Kringle was on his knees, furiously scrubbing the coffee stain on the carpet with a bunched-up paper towel, when SHE walked in.

Colonel Margaret Claus herself.

Kringle jumped to his feet, saluted. Hating himself all the while.

What kind of man kowtows to a ghoul in a red fur suit?

No man at all.

"At ease, Private," Claus said, looking casually around the room before settling in the single desk chair, drawing one knee over the other.

Kringle stood there, crushing the paper towels in his hand, wishing he had a hold of her throat instead.

"I'm told we had an alert?" She cocked her chin at the display.

"Place called Pine Canyon. The Southerlands. California, I believe."

"Hmm." Claus turned to the display, punched in

a code. The computer sprang to life, code scrolling down the screen. She bit her lip, punched more buttons, inspecting the readout. "Oh my."

Kringle tried to blend into the corrugated metal wall. Clauses in general made him sick, but Red Maggie made him positively homicidal.

After all, SHE'D been in charge of the Krampus Corps. She was the one who'd sent his unit into Lollipopland, underprepared and under-armed. The massacre on the beach and every shitty dream he'd had since were entirely her fault.

Not to mention his current gig, freezing his ass off in a Quonset hut and waiting for more Clausian mistakes to rear their ugly heads.

Colonel Claus tapped a few more buttons, sighed, then sat back heavily in her chair. "Well, fuck."

Kringle kept his mouth shut. With any luck, she'd flit away to deal with whatever situation her people created and leave him to his horrible dreams and twelve snowflakes an hour (before taxes).

Claus turned to him. "We've got a situation."

"And?" Clauses ALWAYS had situations.

"And," Colonel Claus said, rising from her chair, "I could use your help."

Kringle tried not to scoff—he didn't need yet another black mark on his record. "Not sure how much help I can be. I'm just a simple Private."

"Please." Colonel Claus crossed the tiny space in an instant, grabbed his elbow. "You were the best we had."

Kringle scowled, turned away. "That was a long time ago."

"Maybe. But when the Halloween King rigged

every Christmas jack-in-the-box with C4, who tracked him down and put a bullet between his eyes?"

Kringle demurred. "Me."

Claus stroked his cheek, her skin soft against his stubble. "And remember when that psychotic chocolate factory owner kidnapped a sleighful of elves, started calling them Humpa-Chumpas? I seem to recall you not only got our elves back, you also threw his ass out of a glass elevator."

"I see what you're doing."

"All I'm DOING," Claus said, leaning into him, "is reminding you of who you are."

Kringle gestured vaguely at the cluttered Quonset hut, redolent of stale air and staler coffee. "This is who I am."

"Is it?" Claus turned suddenly, stepping over to the computer, hips swishing this way and that. "Matt, I won't lie to you. The situation is dire. I need someone with your particular set of skills."

"If you need me so much, why'd you fuck me over? After Lollipopland?"

Colonel Claus shrugged. "Politics? I won't lie to you, that whole fiasco put my career on the line. The Clausian Hegemony wanted SOMEONE'S head, and you were it. Was it wrong? Of course. But I've got a career to think about."

"At least you're honest."

"Hey." Claus ran a hand over her red-furred suit. "How old are you?"

Kringle thought for a moment. "A hundred and forty."

Claus smirked. "That's what I thought. You've lived your whole life without a Santa. Hell, the whole

IDEA of a Santa isn't just theoretical to you at this point. It's a myth. And all this—" she whirled, slowly, hands outstretched, indicating their entire polar existence, "the Clauses and the Kringles, Elftown, presents and lists and reindeer and that one old snowman who won't stop telling boring stories about dentists? None of it makes sense, not without a Santa. We've all been shivering in the cold, waiting for our savior to return, and look where it's gotten us? We're shitting all over the Imagination Accords. Fighting with each other. Hell, the entire Claus/Kringle thing is just a social engineering experiment gone wrong, you know that, right?"

Of course, he knew that. Every Kringle did. Still, didn't make being a second-class citizen any better.

"The old Santas were . . . unenlightened."

Kringle arched an eyebrow. That was borderline apostasy. She was clearly baiting him. Typical Red Maggie bullshit.

"Don't rat me out, okay? Last thing I need is to get fed to a yeti."

For all their technology, some of the laws of the Clausian Hegemony were downright barbaric.

"So, what're you saying?" Kringle finally said. "Shit sucks? Damn straight. I'm sure it sucks for you in ways I can't understand, the same goddamn way YOU will never, ever know what it's like to live your life as a Kringle. What I can't figure out is why you're at my station, feeding me all this bullshit. Whatever this is," Kringle waved vaguely at the display, "it's not my goddamn problem. I'm sure you've got more Krampus Corps squads trained and ready to kill for you."

Claus looked at the floor, grinding the toe of her

white fur-lined boot into the carpet. Inches from the coffee stain he'd been working on, which had faded to near-invisibility. "This, uh, isn't the kind of mission I'd want to dispatch an entire KC contingent for."

Kringle gaped at her for a second, then laughed, something he hadn't done in a VERY long time. "You're screwed."

Claus didn't meet his gaze.

Kringle marched over to the door, wrenched it open. The wind howled, frigid polar air swirled inside the tiny hut. "Get out."

"Matt—"

"Ah, and there it is. *Matt* my ass. You don't want anyone finding out. Can't risk the rest of the fucking Clauses getting wise, probably. Whatever it is, they'll do worse than just feed you to a yeti."

Claus said nothing.

"Lucky for you, old Matt Kringle caught the call. You figured you'd waltz in here with a bunch of sugarplum promises, and I'd come trotting obediently behind you like the goddamn Christmas puppy I've always been, and no one would ever be the wiser. That about the shape of things?"

Claus looked up, and the worst parts of Matt Kringle erupted in joy—she was afraid. No, terrified. He'd hit all the right buttons.

The interior of the Quonset hut was now below freezing, but nothing warmed Matt's heart like seeing Red Maggie scared shitless.

"You're right," she finally said, voice quavering. "About everything. I can't have this getting out, and if I call in the Krampus Corps? Hell, if I ORDER you to handle it, which I could? The Council would find out. Worse, the Acting Santa would find out, and you know how much Noel hates my guts. I'm up against it, Matt, and you're the only one who can help me."

Something inside Kringle softened, just slightly, melting like snow. He nudged the door closed. "What's going on, anyway?"

Claus met his eyes, finally. "Something bad. Something very bad. But if we play this right, we can change everything. Everything."

Kringle stared back at her for a long time. A very long time.

But finally, he said the words he knew he was always going to say, from the minute Red Maggie said she wanted something.

"Tell me."

7:29pm Pacific Standard Time

Not long after itinerant true crime buff Clue Francis shuffled off this mortal coil—or close enough for government work, whatever—a golf cart pulled into the Whosgotta parking lot, laden down with three caroling Christpunks. Caterpillar leaned out the side, pumping his fist to a particularly raucous rendition of "Jingle Bell Rock," brown sludgy droplets spilling from the FOURTH fucking hot chocolate he'd had in the last hour.

"Get back in the ride," Self-Harm grunted, yanking the other boy in by his leather jacket.

Caterpillar scowled. "Don't you have no Christmas spirit, you Scrooge-ass motherfucker?"

"I got Christmas spirit. I got nothing BUT Christmas spirit." Self-Harm thumped a fist against the dash. "Just don't want you knocking your block off, that's all."

"Pssh, ain't nothing gonna knock MY block off, man."

Landfill leaned in from the backseat. "Can you two please shut the fuck up? It's Christmas."

The two boys hung their heads. "You right," Caterpillar said. "Lil Baby Jesus wouldn't want us to be mean to each other." His eyes lit up. "I forgot to tell y'all, I just saw Lil Baby Jesus is playing the Coliseum next week!"

"Isn't he in prison for stabbing a guy at F.A.O. Schwartz?" Landfill scoffed.

"Nah, the only witness disappeared or some shit. Man, I hope he do 'My Christmas Dick.'"

Self-Harm nodded approvingly. "Old school."

"And a one, and a two—"

"My Christmas dick, my Christmas Dick
Green like the Grinch since I stuck dat bitch
Raw-dogged that pussy when I shoulda wrapped my present
Now it burns when I pee like an overcooked pheasant . . . "

They pulled into a parking spot next to the loading dock, Caterpillar still rapping about diseased genitalia and hallowed Yuletide traditions.

"This place looks cool," Self-Harm said.

Caterpillar hopped out, wandering up the loading dock. "Yo, Tommy! Where yo juggalo ass at?"

Silence.

RETURN OF THE LIVING ELVES

The scents of pine and peppermint wafted out of the open bay door. Landfill inhaled deeply, eyes fluttering shut for a moment, the smell bringing back some of her fondest memories—diapered and bow-legged, chasing a model train around the Christmas tree, clapping her hands together in delight. Seated on Santa's lap, whispering an urgent plea for the latest Babsey dream yacht in his hairy ear. Baking cookies with her mom and dad, snow falling gently outside the kitchen window.

Guys like Self-Harm, they were more about the *Christ* than the *mas*. Caterpillar was just along for the ride, half-poser, wearing their lifestyle like a costume since he was addicted to hot chocolate and fast living.

But Landfill?

She motherfucking LOVED Christmas, y'all.

Caterpillar sniffed the air loudly, pointed at the warehouse. "Y'all smell that? Like those Christmas trees they supposably don't sell here." He wagged a finger at Landfill. "I was right, y'all watch out for sap."

Landfill snatched his finger, bending it back nearly to the point of breaking. "Shut up."

"Ow!" Caterpillar yanked his finger away, sucked on it furtively, pausing to scowl at Landfill.

"Man, if Tommy's not here, I say we just go back to Atheist Acres and put a boot up all their asses," Self-Harm sneered. "C'mon, we're burning Yule." The Christpunk stalked into the warehouse, head swiveling from side-to-side.

Landfill rolled her eyes—the guy was so aggro he took an empty loading dock personally, for Frosty's sake—and followed.

"I'm a finish this and be right in," Caterpillar said, shaking his hot chocolate at them.

"Make yourself useful and siphon some gas outta that truck," Self-Harm said. "Golf cart's getting low."

"What, the big rig?"

"No, that's diesel. The other truck." Self-Harm pointed at a rusty Dodge Ram, the only other vehicle in the parking lot. "Hose's in the storage compartment."

"Whatever," Caterpillar said, grabbing the hose and a gas can.

Landfill and Self-Harm left the other Christpunk outside by the big rig and entered the warehouse. The interior was cavernous, eerily silent.

Self-Harm cupped a hand to his mouth, yelled Tommy's name, his voice resounding off the ceiling.

"Huh," Self-Harm said. "THAT'S what my voice sounds like?"

"You've never heard your own voice before?"

"Nah. Pretty sure there's something about that in the Bible."

"There's not."

Self-Harm scratched his ass. "You sure? Because I coulda swore—oh, SHIT!" He suddenly bolted through the aisles, intent on whatever had caught his squirrel-like attention.

Landfill, stuck between the pious meathead and the junkie outside, chose to keep following the former.

Unlike the other Christpunks, she'd actually been in Whosgotta before. Scouted the place out before telling Tommy to apply there, ostensibly to see if they were hiring, but secretly to check out their stash. The manager, a big guy named Jimmy, seemed nice. He gave her an application for her boyfriend and a quick tour. Told her to come back after the holidays when things slowed down, and he'd show her some really cool stuff.

Not in a pervy way, either—even though she'd only spent a couple minutes with the guy, he was clearly a kindred spirit, a devoted lover of the exquisite pleasures the holiday season had to offer.

If only he was a few decades younger—

Self-Harm jumped out from one of the aisles, clutching the biggest snowman Landfill had ever seen. He spun around in a circle, dancing with the plastic decoration.

"SMLCC," Landfill said, nodding. "You've got a good eye, my friend."

"Always wanted one of these!" Self-Harm said, now jumping up and down, the plastic snowman clutched tightly to his chest. "Lookit his nose!" He booped the snowman's snoot, then settled down, leaning against one of the metal shelves, nuzzling his newfound love. "You think I can keep it?"

"Off-season's hours away," Landfill said. "I bet Tommy can work some—"

A gigantic shadow loomed behind Self-Harm. He didn't see it, so intent was he on the object of his affection. "Landfill? You think I should get a corncob pipe? Not to smoke—"

The shadow pounced and bit Self-Harm right on the noggin.

"Ahhhhhh!" Self-Harm screamed. He scrambled to free himself, but the shape hung on tenaciously. Blood poured down his face. He lashed out with a kick, only succeeding in sending his SMLCC spinning off into the darkness. Self-Harm and his attacker stumbled back into the aisles and out of view.

Then silence.

Landfill advanced slowly, heart pounding, mind scrambling to make sense of what she'd just seen.

"Self-Harm? Psst, Self-Harm!"

CRASH!

One of the shelves toppled over, spilling plastic reindeer everywhere. Landfill screamed, falling backwards. The shape who'd attacked her friend advanced, coming into the light—a big guy, wearing blue flannel and jeans, an STP cap on his head.

He kind of looked like a trucker, except what skin she could see was bright green and flaking off his stubbly cheeks. Red eyes the size of softballs bulged out of his sockets. White pus dripped from his nose, his mouth, his ears.

The trucker grinned, showing off four rows of icicle-like teeth.

"Felizzzzzz . . . . Navidad . . . "

Landfill screamed, backpedaled into a half-empty shelf of saxophone-sized novelty candy canes. Thinking quickly, she picked one up and brandished it at the trucker.

"Back off, you hear me? I'll . . . I'll—"

"Grrrraahhh!" The trucker charged.

Landfill stepped to the side and walloped him over the head with the candy cane, which broke immediately because it was made from cheap plastic and definitely NOT up to the task of bludgeoning a ravenous zombie/elf/trucker hybrid.

The creature's momentum carried him into the storage rack, knocking it over, more candy canes raining down to ineffectually pummel his back.

"Hey, y'all found Tommy or what?" a voice called from the loading dock.

The trucker whirled, jaws snapping open, pus flecking off his undulating tongue.

Caterpillar stood silhouetted in the doorway by the parking lot lights, wiping hot chocolate from his mouth with the back of a forearm. His eyes went wide at the sight of the trucker. "Man, what the f—"

The trucker charged, boots slapping heavily across the warehouse floor.

Landfill looked around for a weapon, figured the jagged plastic end of the broken candy cane was probably her best bet, and gave chase.

Caterpillar took two steps back, fell off the loading dock. He rolled away, ran for the golf cart.

The trucker jumped and landed in the parking lot.

Landfill followed, hopping on his back. She stabbed him in the neck. The flesh yielded with surprising ease to the makeshift holiday shiv, skin rending in a jagged line. Blood spurted all over the asphalt.

The trucker bucked and tossed Landfill off. She hit the ground hard, the wind knocked out of her in a single, painful whoosh. Across the parking lot, golf cart tires squealed, Caterpillar yelling "Sorry!" over the slight sound of the electric engine.

Landfill blinked, trying to get her bearings.

A shape loomed over her. The trucker smiled, showing off all those teeth. His breath was fetid, the sweet scent of peppermint undercutting the stench of rot. She gagged, choking back vomit.

"Deeeck . . . the . . . halls . . . "

Panic welled in her chest and Landfill fervently hoped that against all odds she'd not only survive, but this whole bullshit zombie/murder experience wouldn't ruin Christmas for her.

But the pragmatic part of her figured she'd almost certainly be disappointed on both counts.

```
7:32pm Pacific Standard Time
Kaltenbreuer's Brewing Company
```

Ten minutes before clocking out, Louisa broke a pint glass.

She was already pissed, having to work Christmas Eve. Not like she gave a shit—the holidays had never been much fun growing up, since her mother had to work doubles at the massage parlor, sticking her with her grandma, a bitter old *Wheel of Fortune* addict who cared more about cigarettes than grandchildren. Most years they didn't even have a tree, so when she finally moved out and got her own place, well, she was more likely to celebrate Thanksgiving since it was the one fucking day a year her mother didn't make shitty comments about how much she was or wasn't eating.

No, the reason Louisa hated working Christmas Eve was because of the goddamn customers.

Working at a craft brewery nestled in the heart of an industrial park, she had her regulars—dedicated hopheads who obsessed over IPAs—and maybe the occasional cluster of spandex-clad bikers or overgrown frat boys on a party bus. Unlike some of the bars she'd worked in, people were polite, and probably more turned on by exotic hop combinations than her tits.

On Christmas Eve, they were still polite, but everybody was drenched in red and green and goddamn TINSEL, sporting ugly sweaters, fucking SANTA HATS, and she hated every last one of the sons of bitches and couldn't wait till her goddamn shift was over, so she could go home and watch a motherfucking horror movie like God intended.

But then—

SMASH.

Her elbow whacked the last dirty pint on the bar, just a splash of their latest double dry-hopped IPA commingling with dude spit in the bottom, sending it tumbling end-over-end, breaking on the metal edge of the open ice chest. Shattered glass rained like the snowflakes she'd never seen because every last one of her twenty-six years had been spent in Southern California.

"Shit!"

Louisa groaned, peering into the ice chest. She'd held out hope the glass had shattered into big enough pieces she could pick them out, puzzle-piece it back together on the bar for safety's sake, but no. Stupid idea anyway, Ernesta would fucking murder her if one of their customers got internal bleeding, because she was a hardass like that.

Lame.

Grabbing the scoop, Louisa started shoveling ice into the trash can. But it was taking forever. Maybe she could grab a bucket, fill it with hot water? Melt all this shit and then wipe down the inside of the cooler?

DING DING DING, we have a winner!

Louisa pushed through the door into the back, on the hunt for a bucket. She spied one nestled underneath the dish pit. Grabbed it, filled it with hot water. Was walking by Susie's office when she heard a noise.

Louisa frowned. Nobody else was around—rats?

Her skin crawled at the thought.

Holding the bucket, water sloshing from side to side, she approached the door, peering through the smoked glass.

The door was ajar.

Louisa shouldered it open, confident that if a disgusting-ass rat really was poking through her boss's paperwork, she could trap it under the bucket and—hopefully—figure out a way to maneuver it outside. She'd been mostly vegan since two boyfriends ago and didn't want to murder anything unless it had a shitty throat tattoo.

The second the door opened, an odd smell wafted out—peppermint and pine needles, like the one time a different, non-vegan ex dragged her up to Big Bear on the back of his motorcycle. Louisa scrunched up her nose, frowned.

The office LOOKED empty, but that didn't mean anything. It was a small space, cramped, dominated by a big desk and some shelving.

Then, a scuffling noise.

Not from the floor, where she expected a Christmas rat might be creeping about, ready to teach her some esoteric lesson about the true meaning of the holiday she'd bah-humbugged ever since the night her grandmother called the Grinch a name you would most certainly NOT want to utter out loud in Tel Aviv, most parts of Brooklyn, or polite company in general.

No, the sound was coming from much higher.

She looked across the office, to the shelving behind the desk, where Ernesta kept a bunch of antiquated three-ring binders holding brewing recipes she wouldn't trust to a software program.

One of the binders toppled to the ground.

"Hey there, sweetheart," a high-pitched voice said.

Louisa dropped the bucket of hot water, soaking her tennis shoes, because to her astonishment, there was—and I'm sorry, dear reader, so sorry, but I simply cannot help myself—an ELF on the shelf.

The thing was on her before she even had time to scream.

7:36pm Pacific Standard Time

Jimmy lay on the floor, clutching his stomach and groaning.

He felt like his belly was about to burst, his pants had long since split down the middle, and his heart-covered boxers weren't doing so hot, either. Sweat streamed down his forehead.

"Ho, ho, ho," he muttered softly.

What the hell was happening to him?

Jimmy always figured his body was gonna give out on him one of these days, what with the diabetes, and the carpal tunnel, and the way he didn't ever get enough fiber in his diet like his goddamn ex-wife Lorna insisted he needed, pushing bowls of fucking PRUNES at him like he was some old fogey instead of a sprightly fifty-seven and-a-half. What he never figured was his mind going at the same time. Maybe he was having a stroke, whatever that was. He never knew anybody who had one before. His dear old dad got crushed by a shipping container two days before Easter—figure that one out—and his ma, she was the very picture of health until she passed peacefully in her sleep well into her eighties. His family history was barely more than a shrug, one big medical *que sera sera.*

He rubbed his belly. There was so much of it. So, so much of it. He instantly regretted every Meat Blast he'd ever had from Angelo's, even though they had precious little to do with his present condition, since the aged fruitcake of indeterminate origin was the clear culprit.

"Stupid diabetes," Jimmy muttered, somehow managing to get a thought out without ho-ing it up.

Then he heard it. Upstairs.

Voices.

Muted through concrete and steel—or whatever bargain equivalent Roberta's great-grandfather used to build the joint in the first place—Jimmy couldn't make out what they were saying, or who saying it. But there were a couple of 'em, so it couldn't be the elf.

He opened his mouth to yell DOWN HERE—or try—then clamped it shut when he remembered the kid.

Jimmy shot a glance at his former employee—still very dead. Blood covered half his face, clown paint the rest. He was also staring at Jimmy, which was very rude, because Jimmy hadn't wanted to kill him in the first place, and this whole goddamn thing was his fault.

Gently, Jimmy poked the kid's chin with the crowbar until his head lolled to the side, his one wide-open eye now staring at the cement wall for all eternity, or at least until somebody dragged his ass out of the basement.

The voices were saying something else, now. Jimmy still couldn't make heads or tails of it, but figured they had to be a couple Teamsters, wondering where the hell Jimmy was so they could drop off their loads of returned decorations and go the fuck home to their families.

He weighed his options.

On the one hand, he really needed medical attention. Maybe they could pump his stomach, arrest whatever weird condition he'd contracted.

On the other hand, there was that whole dead body thing, plus a psychotic zombie elf that couldn't have been a figment of Jimmy's imagination, because otherwise he'd have beat the kid to death for nothing more than a waking dream, and THAT was the kind of knowledge that'd surely smash his already-frazzled brain into eleventy-billion pieces.

"Ho," Jimmy said quietly, a single tear running down his cheeks, getting lost in the snow-white beard which now hung betwixt his man-tits.

At least his stomach wasn't hurting anymore.

Gingerly, he got to his feet—wasn't actually as hard as he thought it would be, even though he had twice the stomach, he didn't FEEL any heavier. Actually, now that he thought about it, his joints didn't scream in protest like they usually did, and the low-grade mental fog that usually clung to his synapses was gone.

Jimmy felt fresh, alert. Kinda strong, even.

Huh.

He grabbed the crowbar, wiped it a couple more times on the kid's jeans, and then got to work pushing their make-shift barricade aside.

Whatever was happening, he sure as hell wasn't gonna spend Christmas Eve with a dead body.

7:39pm Pacific Standard Time

The zombified trucker snapped its jaws, spewing rancid-yet-sweet breath in Landfill's face.

She swallowed her gorge and stabbed the motherfucker in its eye with her candy cane shiv. Her attacker's head snapped back, the STP cap flew off, sailing away across the parking lot to rest under a truck tire.

The trucker yowled in pain, sickening green hands going to its face. Pus squirted between its fingers, splashing the asphalt.

Landfill cocked back a fist and punched the thing as hard as she could, slamming the plastic shard deep into whatever was left of its brain.

The trucker's yowls cut off immediately, like an unplugged TV. It swayed, crumpled to the ground, luckily landing just inches from Landfill.

"What. The. Fuck."

She lay there on the ground for a long moment,

chest heaving, head spinning. The last couple minutes made zero sense. Less than zero.

Drugs, she thought. Had to be. She'd heard vague stories on the news about truckers and amphetamines, popping pills and snorting powders to make their routes in time. The guy who'd attacked her, and Self-Harm, must've gotten a particularly bad batch, and—

Self-Harm!

Not to mention Tommy, who was presumably somewhere in the warehouse too. Landfill scrambled to her feet, wiping sticky trucker blood on her jeans. Once her hands were clean enough, she pulled her phone from her pocket—totally smashed, the black screen a rizzle-dizzle of cracks. She tried to restart it, but no amount of holding down the side button and screaming "WORK MOTHERFUCKER!" made a damn jingle bell of difference.

Seething with frustration, she chucked the dead phone at the big rig, where it glanced off the side and went spinning into the night and out of this story.

She eyed the dead body—unmoving, thankfully— then glanced at the roll-up door, the dark warehouse beyond. Part of her wanted to run off into the night, find a working phone. Call somebody—*but who,* that pragmatic part of her who'd been so pessimistic about her chances for survival and sustained Yuletide joy asked. The cops? And tell them what, exactly?

She should at least go check to see if Self-Harm was okay.

He's not.

But he was her friend, even though he was gruff and hard to like, and did a terrible job of hiding his unrequited love for her, constantly dropping comments about how she could do so much better than a fucking Juggalo, and wouldn't she be happier with a Christpunk—not HIM, of course, he was Just Saying™—never understanding that Landfill loved the secular aspects of Christmas more than the religious ones, didn't even celebrate Easter, and might've felt more comfortable calling herself an atheist rather than agnostic, if anybody ever asked.

Her and Tommy didn't see eye to eye on everything, she couldn't stand the gross sugary taste of Fanta and cringed whenever he wanted to pour it on her boobs, but Tommy ACCEPTED her and her lifestyle, understood her on a deeper level than she'd ever known possible. Hell, he'd even left Angelo's and got a job at a Christmas supply warehouse, for her.

If that wasn't true love, what the fuck was?

Tommy was in there, somewhere, and if she could find him then they'd figure it all out together, the way they did most things.

Mind made up, she climbed up onto the loading dock.

She paused at the roll-up door, listening.

The night was silent, but not holy. That strange conglomeration of scents still hung in the air, pine and peppermint and rot.

Now mixed with blood.

"Hello? Self-Harm?" Landfill swallowed. "Tommy?"

Nothing.

She looked about for a new weapon, since teasing her crappy plastic shiv out of the dead trucker's eye didn't seem worth it. They had to have all kinds of stuff in the warehouse she could use—maybe a shepherd's crook made from real wood for that nativity scene veracity, or a particularly hefty Angelic tree-topper.

But all that stuff was further back in the warehouse, and she had no reason to think the psycho trucker was alone. Maybe there was a whole gaggle of them, creeping along the rafters, staring at her right now.

She glanced up at the ceiling, thirty feet above her head. Too dark to see anything. She felt around for a switch on the wall. Her finger brushed against it after a minute, she flipped it on, fluorescent light fixtures springing to life.

Her pulse slowed, slightly—now the interior of Whosgotta just looked like a warehouse full of Christmas cheer again, albeit a very messy one. Maybe it really was just a single, drug-addled trucker.

"S.H., can you hear me?"

Something clinked over near the aisle where he'd fallen, followed by a soft noise that might've been a moan.

He's alive!

Forgetting her trepidation, Landfill ran towards the noise. She vaulted over a box of spilled mistletoe and rounded the corner, relieved her friend was still kicking. Grievously wounded, most likely, but at least there was a chance—

She staggered to a halt.

Self-Harm was gone.

A bloody stain marred the concrete floor where he'd fallen, alongside some grey and white bits she didn't care to inspect TOO closely. This was definitely the spot, she hadn't gotten turned around.

Must've gotten up, she thought. Which meant he was ambulatory. Which meant his wounds couldn't be nearly as bad as she first thought.

A Christmas miracle!

"Yo, Self-Harm!" Landfill called again. "Where're you at?"

Her eyes flicked back to the stain on the floor. There really was a LOT of blood. Then again, she didn't know how much blood people had, or if a big guy like Self-Harm had extra. They never taught her stuff like that in school.

Landfill frowned, turning in a slow circle, listening for more moans, footsteps, anything. "Self—"

The other Christpunk jumped out from behind a shelf, grabbing her by the throat, pushing her up against a toppled crate.

Landfill grabbed his wrists, tried to rip his fingers away, but he was too strong. She struggled in his grasp.

Unlike the trucker, Self-Harm's skin wasn't an ooey gooey green, but it had a weird tint to it, and his breath just stank like stale hot chocolate and half-assed dental care. But the flesh around his forehead was all chewed up, his face was streaked with blood, and his eyes were dull, dead. A tiny dollop of pinkish brain matter fell from his exposed skull and splatted on the floor.

Self-Harm leaned in and slowly licked her cheek. "Come on, baby, it's cold outside," he murmured in her ear.

Landfill kneed him in the balls.

Self-Harm made a soft *oof* noise and let go, hands going to his crotch, face screwed up in pain.

That a nut-shot bothered him, while his much-more-gnarly head wound did not, confirmed all sorts of suspicions Landfill long harbored about her "friend."

Landfill grabbed the closest thing at hand—a ceramic gingerbread house—and smashed it over Self-Harm's head. He crumpled to the ground, moaning, then crawled across the floor in a bloody circle, leaving the world's most disgusting snail-trail in his wake.

She looked about for another weapon—more plastic crap.

"Stay down," she yelled. "Don't make me hurt you again."

Self-Harm groaned in response, bumping head-first into the metal shelving. He grabbed the shelf, pulling himself up to his feet.

"Never shoulda dated a Juggalo," Self-Harm said bitterly, his words almost unintelligible through the blood and phlegm and gruesome head injury. "Christpunks belong with our own. It—" He doubled over in a coughing fit, yellow sputum splodging the ground. He wiped a hand across his mouth, then whipped his head around, jaw outstretched, skin greening, twisted teeth wriggling out of his gums. "It's UNNATURAL!"

Self-Harm threw himself at her like she was the last sugarplum danish in the Starbucks display case.

Landfill turned and ran, banging her hip painfully on the shelving. She rounded the corner, nearly tripping over his beloved SMLCC, and made for the loading dock, pumping her arms as hard as she could.

Self-Harm's heavy boots clomp-clomping behind

BRIAN ASMAN

her all the while, like the world's most inconsiderate reindeer prancing on a rooftop.

Getting closer.

The dark rectangle of the loading dock door seemed too far away, and he was just on her heels. She'd never make it—

Then she saw the barrel full of snow shovels, casually pushed up against the wall.

Passing the barrel, Landfill grabbed a handle and wrenched one free, then dove forward, tucking and rolling with the shovel clutched tightly in her hands, landing in a crouch and simultaneously twisting around, swinging the shovel with all her might.

BRRRRRRRRRRRRANGG!

She nailed Self-Harm dead in the face. He spun away, landing heavily on the floor, while the blade of the shovel vibrated like a tuning fork; a strong, powerful dissonant note buzzing in her ears, echoing throughout the warehouse.

Landfill stood, shovel at the ready.

Self-Harm pushed himself up to hands and knees, more dollops of brain matter leaking out of his skull.

Evidently not the cells that'd harbored his pervy ass crush on her.

He must've noticed her shadow looming over him, because he turned slightly, looking up at her, a slack expression on the remains of his face. "Landfill. Plea—"

"HOME ALONE, MOTHERFUCKER!"

She laid into him with the shovel, smashing his head again and again, knocking him flat on his stomach, then switched her grip, raising the shovel high above her head. Brought the blade down on the back of Self-Harm's neck.

SPPPLUCH!

Landfill jabbed him again, and again, slamming the snow shovel into his neck. Blood flew everywhere, crimson droplets spattering her cheeks. The zombified Christpunk writhed, limbs flailing uselessly.

Landfill stomped on his back, bore down with the shovel, face straining with effort. She let out a scream and then—with a soft, anticlimactic PLOP—Self-Harm's head separated from his body and rolled away down the aisle, coming to a rest next to a boxed train set.

"Choo-choo, asshole," Landfill said, wiping the snow shovel off on Self-Harm's still-twitching legs.

Somebody whistled over to her left, then said, "Nothing gets the job done like a Super-Scoop 700."

Landfill whirled, blood-flecked shovel cocked.

A man stood in the shadows, maybe twenty feet away. She couldn't see much, other than a sizable belly and a snow-white beard glinting in the darkness.

"Come on out of there, now!" Landfill called. "Or else I'm gonna—"

"Easy, now," the man said, stepping into the light, both hands up like her snow shovel was actually a .357 Magnum.

Landfill gaped at him. She dropped the shovel, which hit the ground with such a clatter, but she didn't even notice.

Because a few feet away, standing under the brutal and unforgiving warehouse lights, holding a crow bar and wearing nothing but a stained, too-small blue shirt and white boxers dotted with red hearts?

Was Santa Claus.

7:42pm Pacific Standard Time

The noise. The lights. The sounds of merriment and Yuletide cheer!

All of it drew Elfphonso from the shadows. He followed the music—"We Wish You a Merry Christmas," albeit an arrangement he was not familiar with—to a large, concrete structure the size of a city.

In the furthest reaches of his desiccated, rotten mind, did he still remember Elftown, the place of his birth? The only home he knew, until some Clauses in white coats snatched him off the street, threw him in the back of a black sleigh with tinted windows, and carried him off to their secret laboratory to turn him into a perverse monument against elfkind and nature?

Who's to say, dear reader, who's to say?

Elfphonso wandered through the structure, squinting at the onslaught of light from all the glowing signs. Forever 21. Armani. Build-A-Bear Workshop. He wasn't sure what any of the words meant, but he did know one thing for sure.

He was surrounded by potential conscripts for his army.

Exercising the utmost self-control—he didn't want to start a panic, after all—Elfphonso ambled through the mall, sticking to the shadows, trying his elfy best to come up with a plan. Maybe he could slip into one of the busier shops, the Apple Store, perhaps, and find a way to block the doors. Then dart in and out from under the tables, nipping ankles at his leisure.

The plan seemed promising. He was about to enter the store when a noise distracted him. A familiar sound, one that made his greenish elf-blood boil with rage.

"HO, HO, HO!"

Elfphonso's cute-ish, kinda gross TBH elf-face wrinkled in fury and surprise. While he had no idea where he was, the last thing he expected to find there was HIM.

Dodging between the legs of last-minute shoppers, the elf rounded the next corner, coming into a large courtyard, and gasped. The biggest Christmas tree he'd ever seen, larger even than the Ur-Tree growing in the heart of the Santadel in Vaticlaus City, presided over the scene, draped in garlands and ornaments, fake snow, crowned with a glowing angel he might have recognized as beloved Oscar-winning actor Tom Hanks, if he hadn't been trapped in a snow globe for the last half-century, missing The Burbs, Joe Vs. the Volcano, Catch Me If You Can, Apollo 13, Forrest Gump, and Castaway, plus the latter's AVP-winning porn parody Assaway, which featured noted adult entertainment impresario Axel Braun tenderly fucking a beach ball for two hours.

Beneath the tree sat an ornate golden throne with crimson satin cushions, and on those cushions rested a butt Elfphonso thought long-dead.

A chill—yes, a CHILL—shivered down his foot-long spine.

The Santa Claus.

The Emir of the Reindeer, the Pharaoh of the Snow, the Król of the Pole, the supreme tyrant of Christmasland himself. Oppressor of elfkind and moralistic judgy-pants of children everywhere.

Here? What could the Santa be doing HERE?

Elfphonso stumbled closer, drawn by the natural magnetism that allowed the first Santa to conquer all the Pole-peoples in the first place. Wide-eyed, like a child on Christmas morning, mind unable to process the information streaming in through his eyeballs.

Or eyeBALL, in Elfphonso's case.

Elfphonso didn't stop until he ran right into a kid in a Paw Patrol shirt.

"Hey, watch it," the kid said, then turned back to the line, anxiously rubbing his hands together.

"Sorry," Elfphonso muttered.

He looked around—somehow, he'd accidentally joined the queue, where a curious ritual was taking place. One at a time, children would climb onto the Santa's lap. Words would pass between them—he couldn't hear, so whether the children were pledging fealty to the Santa, or begging for their lives, he didn't know—and then one of the assistants, a human decked out in the most grotesquely offensive and parodical elf-face Elfphonso could imagine, would snatch the child off the Santa's lap, send it waddling off towards its parents.

Only one thing made sense.

The Santa hadn't been assassinated by a radical Lollipoplander or departed the Pole for parts unknown in a bid to find meaning in his immortal existence. No, he'd come south, to conquer. The meaning of the odd tableau suddenly clicked into place—the Santa was clearly building an army. Perhaps to aid him in his bid to conquer the Southerlands, or to re-invade Lollipopland one final time with enough strength to displace the Licorice Queen and psychotic consort, Colonel Mallomar Quataffy.

"Okay, kid, ya ready to meet Santy-Claus?" One of the human helpers leaned down to talk to him, hands on hips. Nose wrinkling at the smell.

Before Elfphonso could reply, the offensively-clad man picked him up and carried him the remaining ten feet to the throne, plunking the elf down in the Santa's lap.

Elfphonso swallowed and stared up into the face of the enemy, ready to beg for mercy.

"Please, sir—"

"Ho, ho, ho, little—uh, boy? What would you like for Christmas?" The Santa turned to one of his assistants. "This one of them Make-a-Wish Kids?"

The assistant shrugged.

"Huh," the Santa said. "Looks like he shot his eye out."

Elfphonso frowned, peering up at the Santa. Something wasn't right. The heady scent of gingerbread that usually accompanied any close encounter with Clauskind was absent. Instead, the man smelled more like sugarplum liquor.

"Hey, kid? Talk to me. We got a line."

Elfphonso's mind reeled. He'd gotten it all wrong. This wasn't the Santa, or even a Claus. Just a sad, drunken man made up to look like him, for reasons Elfphonso wasn't entirely clear on. Some ritual, perhaps?

"Hey, earth to—what's your name, anyway? Whose kid is this?"

It suddenly occurred to Elfphonso that his initial assessment of the situation was correct. The man made up to look like the Santa WAS in fact building an army.

He just didn't know it yet.

"Somebody get this space case off my lap," the Santa snarled at his assistants.

One of them adjusted his stocking cap and took a step towards the throne.

Elfphonso sunk his four rows of teeth into the Santa's wrist and waited for the screams to start.

9:47pm Central Standard time

Thousands of feet below, the heavily-forested northern Canadian wilderness zipped by in a frosty white blur.

Matt Kringle and Margaret Claus were in a stealth sleigh, painted blue-black, pulled by coal-rubbed reindeer, and not a red nose among them. Colonel Claus had changed into a fur-lined flight suit, while Kringle was in his Christmas-camo BDUS—patterns of holly, snowflakes and Douglas firs covered the pants and jacket—hair pulled back with a black bandana.

"So, what's REALLY going on?" Kringle asked.

Colonel Claus looked like she'd just been asked if she'd been a good girl this year. "I told you."

"You really think your tinsel doesn't crinkle," Kringle said, shaking his head. "I buy the Elf Improvement Project. Those spooky bastards over at NPAWS—" or the North Pole Advanced Weaponry Section, to unpointed ears, "are always getting up to stupid shit. You really thought you could create a race of undead elves to save money on labor?"

"They're always getting caught in the machinery. We lose a few hundred a week during the busy season."

Kringle smirked. "And of course, designing a safer work environment never occurred to you."

Claus shrugged. "They're elves."

"Tell you what, after Lollipopland, wasn't a Kringle in Peppermint Park who wanted a goddamn thing to do with me. On top of that, I was flat broke. Spent a lotta time in Elftown." He fixed her with a steely glare. "Guess you could say it gave me perspective. Made me appreciate them. The elves."

"You're a regular St. Nick."

A cloud passed over Kringle's face. "Not after the shit you made me do." They came down over the Rockies, passing into the U.S. Flatlands opened up beneath the sleigh. Woods and meadows passing in the blink of an eye.

"Keep telling yourself that," Claus replied. "And don't you dare bring up that old refrain about how there's no opportunities for Kringles in Peppermint Park other than sleigh maintenance and hosing dead elves out of the gears."

Kringle stood quickly, the sleigh rocking under his weight. Claus grabbed hold of the side.

"Watch it. You need me. I don't need you. I could

bail out right now. File my ears down, set up shop in some human village. Elves taught me how to cobble, I got skills."

Claus put a hand on his knee. "Matt, I'm sorry, okay? Old habits. Clauses are very . . . unforgiving. If you don't keep your tongue sharp, they'll eat you alive."

The muscles in Kringle's neck bulged, his eyes smoldered, and for a moment he thought about grabbing Red Maggie by the under-fur and tossing her ass over the side.

The sight of her spiraling towards the ground, the bells on her flight suit jingling all the way, was enough to sustain him.

For the moment.

"Okay," Kringle said slowly. "But if you want me to help you, you gotta be straight with me. What're we actually chasing? How is this gonna change everything? And finally—" Kringle pointed at the satchel on her hip, "—what's that flashlight-looking thing I saw you slip into your bag back at base?"

The wind rushed by outside the sleigh. Lights on the horizon presaged their imminent arrival in human civilization.

Claus nodded, more to herself than Kringle. Finally said, "This stays between you, me and the reindeer, yes?"

A joke—talking reindeer were strictly a Hollywood invention. The highly-motile ennead pulling their sleigh might've been able to defy gravity but were only as smart as regular reindeer.

Kringle motioned for her to go ahead.

And she did. Laid it out for him, in detail. More than just the EIP—the bait and switch approach they'd use to recruit elven "volunteers," the half-dozen Claus scientists they'd liquidated when the test subjects broke out and infected them with peppermint-flavored venom.

She also told him about the FIELD experiments, conducted in places called Pittsburgh and Louisville, which went even worse.

"We cleaned it up quietly," Claus said. "Captured every last subject and globed them."

"And then you lost 'em."

"Typical fuckup. Signals got crossed and one of the crates disappeared. Haven't heard a thing about it in twenty-five years. Not till tonight, when our satellites picked up a breach."

Kringle smiled, or rather bared his teeth. "And now you've got to clean up the mess before every entity this side of Lollipopland finds out you violated the Imagination Accords. I'm sure Piotr Cottontailvna will be especially displeased, after the Hegemony wouldn't let him stash eggs in Siberia anymore."

"Smirk all you want," Claus said firmly. "If news of this gets out, we'll have a full-blown war on our hands. Maybe with the humans."

"They don't even know we exist."

Claus looked at her feet.

"Great."

"Their technology has improved quite a bit over the past 1600 years. We've had a few talks with their leadership. Officially, the policy is detente. They've got their own problems to deal with, and are afraid of what might happen if the general public became aware of OUR existence. Might undermine their own systems of social control."

"What it's all about," Kringle sneered.

"And they've got nukes, too," Claus said. "If they find out about the previous test runs, we're in for a White Christmas."

The sleigh zoomed over a city. Kringle checked the display—a couple hundred miles out from Pine Canyon, they'd be there in minutes.

"So, nobody in the Hegemony knew what you were up to, and if it gets out, everybody dies. You really fucked up, Maggie," he said, more exhausted than angry. Typical Claus bullshit, once again. Big fucking surprise. "One thing—what's with that device in your satchel?"

Claus bit her lip. "The Elf Improvement Plan wasn't the only genetic engineering initiative."

7:49pm Pacific Standard Time

"Santa?" the girl said uncertainly, staring at Jimmy.

All concerns about having a stroke or otherwise losing his mental faculties slipped his mind—clearly the girl was seeing the same weird, impossible shit he was.

Or there was something in the air, or he was hallucinating HER, or—

"You're real, right?" Jimmy asked.

The girl—blonde, compact, wearing some weird getup and sporting a haircut that shoulda cost her stylist her license, in Jimmy's opinion—frowned at him. "Why wouldn't I be?"

"I dunno," Jimmy said, stepping further out of the

shadows, but taking care not to startle her—she was the only person he'd seen in the last however-long who didn't look all elfy, and that was VERY promising. "Stuff's been weird, lately. I, uh—" now he was close enough to get a good look at her, and damned if she didn't look familiar, "—I know you from somewhere?"

The girl looked him up and down, then her own eyes went wide in surprise. "Jimmy, right? Why're you dressed up like Santa? And—if you don't mind me saying—holy shit, you've put on some weight."

Jimmy shrugged—the sudden weight gain was now the least of his current worries, although he didn't care to think what his tailor bill was gonna look like—and scratched his chin. "Wait," he said, wagging a finger at her, "You're the girl who came in here asking for an application for her boyfriend."

"That's me," the girl replied. "Say, where IS Tommy?"

Jimmy blinked, brain working overtime to reconcile the bubbly, excitable girl who'd been wearing a cute Christmas sweater covered in puppies (who were wearing tiny Christmas sweaters themselves) he'd recently met with the punked out street urchin standing over a headless corpse, asking about a different corpse.

"You're Landfill, huh?" he asked, while his mental rolodex whispered the name she'd given him during the tour—*Linnea*.

Landfill nodded.

"Sorry about my pants," Jimmy muttered, craning his neck to inspect the corpse. "Who the hell's that guy?"

"Self-Harm."

"Why's he called that?"

"That's his Christpunk name. His real name's Mark."

Jimmy waggled his eyebrows. "I can see why he changed it. Who names their kid Mark? Other than normal people."

"Please," Landfill said, "a little respect for the dead?" She covered her mouth, turned away.

"Yeah, okay," Jimmy said. "What're you doing here? And what happened to him?"

Landfill filled him in on the broad strokes—how they'd stopped by to see Tommy, the trucker, Self-Harm's transformation.

"What's going on here, anyway?" Landfill asked. "What's wrong with these guys?"

"Hold on." Jimmy waddled over to the roll-up door, crowbar in hand. Looked around for that little elf fuck, but there was just a dead trucker with a candy cane shiv stuck through his eye lying prone under the sodium lights. "Fucking A, and what happened to HIM?"

Landfill joined him at the door, snow shovel still in hand, regarding the corpse. After a long moment, one where Jimmy found himself overly-acquainted with every drop of blood spreading on the pavement, she asked, "Where's Tommy?"

Jimmy yanked on his beard—one good thing about whatever the hell happened to him, the facial hair was great for nervous tics.

"So, uh, yeah . . . " Jimmy managed, looking down at his shoes, which were the only item of clothing on his body that wasn't strained to the breaking point by his instant weight gain.

"Jimmy? Where IS he?" She looked at him expectantly for what felt like a goddamn eternity.

He didn't reply. Couldn't reply. Just tugged that stupid beard.

Something finally shifted in the girl's expression. She let out a sob and walked away, back into the warehouse. She sat down heavily next to a stray SMLCC, buried her face in its plastic bosom.

The sight about broke Jimmy's heart.

"Hey now," he said, joining her on the floor. "There was nothing I could do, you know?"

"Oh, god . . . " She looked up, tears streaking her makeup. "Are you sure? That he's . . . y'know."

Jimmy felt a little verklempt himself. He laid a paternal hand on her shoulder. "Sorry, darling."

"What happened? Was it—" She gestured at the dead trucker.

The crowbar felt gross and slick in his hand, but Jimmy forced himself to nod. "Yep. Trucker got him."

More than just a white lie, but the truth would benefit no one, so Jimmy just told himself that was what happened and after a minute he kind of believed it, too.

A new round of wails, sobs, and assorted wounded-animal noises erupted from the girl. Jimmy sat there, feeling incredibly uncomfortable, wishing he could do something. The whole thing started because he'd been trying to help the kid give her a Christmas present. Now he wished he could give her, and especially the poor, dead kid, a different present.

A complete do-over.

But failing that, he really wished he could make her feel better about the whole thing, at least stop crying for a bit, because a bunch of crazy shit was going on and as long as that little asshole elf was running around biting people's ankles, they weren't safe, were probably in a whole bunch of danger and didn't even realize it, and should probably work together or something to make sure—

Landfill abruptly stopped crying. One minute the waterworks were going full blast, the next?

Totally calm.

Her eyes were still red, her face streaked with mascara, and when she spoke there was a hitch in her voice, but also a steely calm, like she'd suddenly made her peace with the whole thing.

"We need to call the police."

"Holy shit, you're right." Jimmy hadn't even thought about it. There was the small problem of what to say, but even if they thought he was yanking their collective chain, they'd still send out somebody to give him a stern talking to, or at least a ticket for wasting everyone's time, and then he could show 'em the bodies—

"I dunno if that's such a good idea," Jimmy said.

"Why?"

Jimmy gestured vaguely at the loading dock. "Something I saw on TV. If you got a bunch of dead bodies and a bunch of murder weapons with your fingerprints on 'em, you maybe don't want to call the police."

"The guys I killed got green skin and four rows of teeth."

"That's fair. Okay, you wanna call 'em?"

"My phone broke. You got one?"

"My cell's dead, forgot the charger." Jimmy rose,

his joints actually not popping for once. "There's a landline in the office." He extended a hand to Landfill, but she brushed him off.

The girl dabbed at her face with the hem of her shirt, smearing it with makeup and tears, but she seemed to be much more together than just a few minutes before. "Let's go."

They moved into the office. Jimmy gestured to the spare chair—old habits—and surreptitiously hid the kid's application under a stack of yellowing invoices. The girl sat like a little kid, drawing her knees into her chest and hugging them tight.

Jimmy picked up the receiver, punched in 911.

BRAMP! BRAMP! BRAMP!

He frowned. "It's busy."

Landfill frowned at the receiver, then untucked her legs and crossed over to the little black and white TV on top of an overstuffed file cabinet. She flipped it on.

A grainy image of the Yule Log filled the screen.

They both silently basked in the mundanity of corporate-sponsored Christmas cheer for a long moment, before she flipped to the news.

"Uh-ho," Jimmy said.

8:17pm Pacific Standard Time

We go now to the KRGL Evening Broadcast, already in progress:

"—turning the Haskins' family Christmas HAM into a Christmas SHAM."

"Boy, you just can't make this stuff up, can you, Joan?"

"You sure can't, Lucas." Joan turned to the camera, a grave expression settling over her face. A BREAKING NEWS chevron appeared at the bottom of the screen. "Now in local news, there seems to be a riot happening right now at the Nunez Square Mall."

Lucas put on a concerned-yet-moralistic expression and shook his head slowly. "Incredible, Joan, just incredible. Seems like every year a fight breaks out between two parents over the latest, hottest toy. Turbo-Man, Tackle Me Ermo. And we've just gotten used to it."

"Real shame, Lucas. Let's go to Mark Philbin with the KRGL eye in the sky. Mark, what do you see up there?"

The screen cut to a middle-aged man in a chopper, hovering over the mall. Below, several fires had broken out, and even several hundred feet in the air, one could still hear the screams and shattering glass.

"It's real bad down there," Philbin yelled over the hum of the rotors. "Police are setting up a barricade around the whole mall."

"Any word on what kicked off this whole mess?" Joan asked. "And, more importantly, does P.J. Zazzles have any more Tackle Me Ermos in stock?"

"Sorry, Joan," Philbin said. "My sources on the ground are reporting P.J. Zazzles is SOLD OUT of Tackle Me Ermos. I repeat, they are OUT of Tackle Me Ermos. The toy department clerk is currently hiding in a storage closet and checking in with the Hemdale location. Wait, what?" Philbin clamped his hand over his ear. "I'm hearing the Hemdale location is out too. Repeat, do NOT go to Hemdale."

RETURN OF THE LIVING ELVES

"Thanks, Mark," Joan said. "We'll be following the Nunez Mall riots closely all night, as well as those very concerning Tackle Me Ermo shortages." She flipped to a more upbeat expression. "And now, a real life Christmas Carol! He used to be a miser, but local businessman Don Gallagher is warming hearts this holiday seasons with his Candy for Cripples drive—"

"Oh, fuck!" Philbin yelled.

Joan's face froze—total glitch in the Matrix-style—then eked out a tiny smile. "Mark, we can't have—"

The producer, knowing a good story when he heard one, FCC rules be damned, cut over to the chopper video feed.

Just in time to see the whole picture tilt sideways as the pilot tried, and unfortunately failed, to dodge what looked to the wondering eyes of WKRGL's entire extended viewership like a MOTHERFUCKING FLYING SLEIGH.

Oh, snap.

8:19pm Pacific Standard Time

They advanced, a strange and disorganized wave, spilling out of the mall's twelve main entrances. Some still carried the vestiges of the evenings they were supposed to have—folded-up jackets tucked under their arm, weighted-down shopping bags swinging from their green, veiny hands. Others were in varying stages of undress, as they'd been bitten while trying on Christmas sweaters or fancy new jeans.

Or banging in the breakroom, like the Miracle Nacho clerk—Stanley from his nametag—wandering past the elevator, pants around his ankles, the remnants of his half-chewed member swinging in the wind.

At the vanguard, riding atop the shoulders of a zombified volunteer dressed up as the Santa himself, was Elfphonso. Barking orders, urging his newly-minted army on.

Grinning with satisfaction, as the world was now his. Or soon would be.

"Onward, my minions! Onward! Hahaha!"

EMS vehicles squealed into the parking lot, stopping short at the sight of the horde. A confused cop yelled something inaudible into his radio, then was overtaken, his flesh ripped apart by hungry mouths.

The less said about what happened to the paramedics, the better.

Overhead, a helicopter briefly circled, then was obliterated in a flash of light by some unseen and totally fucking unidentified flying object. Debris rained down, a falling rotor chopped one of the elfwear-clad assistants in half.

Blood splatted Elfphonso's cheeks. Fire danced in his eyes. Hunger and rage coursed through his tiny body.

Then he looked up and nearly made poo-poo in his elf-pants.

Pinwheeling through the sky, sloughing off flaming helicopter bits with every herky-jerky motion, was a now totally-identified object.

A C-280 Stealth Sleigh.

The sleigh spiraled, careening over the fence hemming in the parking lot, skipping over the tree line before finally crashing just out of sight. Fire erupted from the impact, a blazing column rushing skyward.

The crash did nothing to assuage Elfphonso's fraying nerves.

Even if the occupants didn't survive—questionable, since the C-280s were fully loaded with all manner of safety features, and both Clauses and Kringles were genetically-engineered marvels, able to withstand the extreme polar temperatures—the sight told him he had very little time left.

The Clausian Hegemony had found him.

Elfphonso yanked the fake Santa's ear, directing him towards one of the abandoned ambulances.

8:27pm Pacific Standard Time

In a nondescript suburban neighborhood semi-adjacent to the Nunez Mall, the Streiner family slept peacefully. Bob in his easy chair, face covered in chocolate hazelnut spread from a massacred platter of leftover hors d'euvres. Stacy in the master bedroom they'd rarely shared over the last three months, also passed out early with a half-empty wine bottle on the nightstand.

And finally little Russell, tucked safe and sound in his racecar bed, a stocking cap on his head, because IMAGERY IS GOD MOTHERFUCKER.

Russell's tiny little nose twitched, he kicked in his sleep like a puppy, and maybe, just maybe, he was dreaming of the most perfect Christmas morning one can imagine—steaming mugs of hot cocoa, stuffed stockings filled with goodies, and, most importantly, all those tantalizing PRESENTS under the tree, stacked so high you could barely see the Star Wars Rebels ornaments hanging from the pine needles.

Let's hope he was, dear reader, because just as his little pajama-wrapped foot kicked the covers, 3,000 pounds of Clausian defense tech came crashing down on the Streiner family's abode, reducing Bob, Stacy, and even little Russell himself to a flaming pile of ash.

Not even the chocolate chip cookies, so hopefully left on a decorative plate emblazoned with one of Norman Rockwell's finest depictions of wholesome mid-century Americana, survived the firestorm.

8:32pm Pacific Standard Time

Smoke.

Fire.

Blood.

The sickening miasma swirled in Matt Kringle's senses. Ichor ran down the side of his face. He touched his cheek, seeking the source of the wound. Found a nasty cut in his scalp—probed it, his stomach turning, but it seemed shallow enough. He groped in the smoky darkness, looking for something to staunch the flow, before he simply readjusted the bandana around his head.

Good enough for government work.

He groaned and pushed himself up into a sitting position. Memories flooded back, swift and mean and fast—that human helicopter came out of NOWHERE! Seriously, that pilot should lose his fucking license, except he was almost certainly dead. Despite the advanced airframe of the C-280, the collision destroyed the rotors, set the engines aflame, and squashed at least half the reindeer. Red Maggie tried her best to get it under control, but they were spinning, hurtling to earth, and there wasn't a damn thing Kringle could do but launch himself over the side and hope he remembered to tuck and roll when he hit the ground.

The impact was the last thing he remembered.

He looked around, trying to get his bearings. A blazing fire drew his attention—the sleigh had crashed into a house, or what used to be a house, because now it was just a burning pile of wrecked lumber. The C-280 was clearly done for, along with the rest of the reindeer.

He could hear their screams on the wind as they burned.

Lights came on in nearby houses, people came out onto front porches, pushed drapes aside to peek through windows.

"FUBAR," Kringle muttered—the elf shit was bad enough but crashing a sleigh on human territory was a clear violation of the Imagination Accords.

Red Maggie had really done it this time.

Speaking of, Kringle struggled to his feet—

unsteady—and looked around. He didn't see her anywhere.

"You okay, buddy?" a guy in a Dodgers hat with heavily-inked arms asked.

Kringle waved him off, and there must've been something of the old Krampus Corps Black Ops SOB in his eyes, because Dodgers Cap fucked off right quick, backing away until he disappeared behind a lifted truck in his driveway.

Stealth was out the window—hell, the whole damn mission was—so Kringle cupped a hand to his mouth and called, "Colonel!"

The night was quiet, except for the sounds of sirens in the distance, the pop and crackle of the blazing Streiner house, the screaming, dying reindeer, and the thumping of his own heart.

And then—

"Matt!" a voice called.

Weakly.

Kringle spun around, trying to locate the sound. She followed up his name with a bunch of phlegmy coughs, which helped a lot. He crossed the yard of a neighboring house, away from the fire, and that's where he found her.

Impaled on the bayonet of a 10-foot tall Nutcracker.

The blade stuck up through her chest, her legs wriggled uselessly while her head hung back, body bent in a U-shape. A disturbing amount of blood pooled in the fake snow beneath her. Her red-and-white cap had fallen off, her blonde hair long and loose and shining in the moonlight.

Kringle had spent many a lonely polar night

imagining all manner of horrific ends for Red Maggie, but now that he was bearing witness to that very thing?

He didn't feel much of anything at all.

Red Maggie sucked in a breath as blood ran down the sides of her mouth. "Matt . . . I . . . " She tried to say something else, but it was lost in a coughing fit.

Kringle approached the dying Claus. He gave her wound a cursory inspection—nothing he could do. She'd lost too much blood already.

"I called 911!" some woman yelled from behind him. He raised a hand to silence her.

Kringle leaned in close to Red Maggie. "It's all fucked. Just another Lollipopland, right?"

She tried to laugh, but lost it in another coughing fit, spraying a fine red mist up at the heavens. Flecks alighted on his cheeks, turning them a pleasant rosy-red.

He should've been gloating, reveling in the bloody comeuppance finally, fucking FINALLY delivered to that rancid ghoul.

But he wasn't.

A single tear slid down his cheek. He wiped it away reflexively, bit his lip.

"We're all screwed," she managed. "The Council will call in a White Christmas, and then that egg-laying sack of shit Piotr Cottonailovna will have a goddamn field day. Not to mention the humans. Ever since they got the bomb, we've known it could come to this, but—" she trailed off again, no coughing this time, just a sad, still look in her eyes.

Kringle thought she was dead already, just for a moment, but then she gripped his forearm with the sort of strength only the dying possess.

"Matt," she said, so soft he had to lean right next to her mouth, feel her breath on his ear—warm, normal, painfully normal—"listen to me."

Kringle'd spent his whole damned life listening to Clauses, and this is where it'd gotten him. But still.

Maybe it was habit. Conditioning. Or maybe, just maybe, he heard something in Red Maggie's voice he never expected to hear.

Honesty.

Whatever it was, when she reached into her red fur flight suit, hand shaking, and pulled out that strange flashlight-like device and pressed it into his hand? Explained exactly what he needed to do with it, and how it could turn the tide, right every wrong in their entire fucked up existence? Rebalance the scales between Clauses and Kringles, and maybe even elves, too?

Like she'd said back in the Quonset hut, they could change EVERYTHING.

For once in his life, Matt Kringle actually BELIEVED a Claus.

Not just obeyed, but believed.

He held her hand tightly as she shuddered her last breath, and even pressed his lips gently to hers, all the hate frozen away in a night colder than any he'd experienced at the North Pole.

When the fire trucks pulled onto the street, he slipped away through the shadows, the miracle device clutched tightly to his chest.

Wondering what might've been, if either of them had been born different.

RETURN OF THE LIVING ELVES

`9:59pm Rocky Mountain Standard Time`

Another phone call, another bunker.

Another beleaguered working stiff in a rumpled uniform discarding a well-loved copy of Penthouse (June 2012, featuring the lovely and probably also-talented Alexis Ford), gingerly zipping up the fly of his BDUs, and holding a receiver to his lantern jaw.

"NORAD, Private Drake speaking."

The voice on the other end was frantic, garbled. Drake figured it was some kinda prank. Ever since they started doing that bullshit Santa tracker on the nightly news, there was always some enterprising teen who went through his brigadier general father's shit and found the dispatch office's number. Got their kicks from harassing the hardworking men and women of America's first and best line of defense against a nuclear-powered sucker punch.

Then Drake heard one word, loud and clear.

Yinzer.

"Please hold! Like, seriously, please." Drake gave his Penthouse Pet a quick file-folder cover-up and hit the intercom. "Sergeant Brice! Get in here, now!"

Seconds later, the door burst open. Brice, a large man who bore a striking resemblance to William "The Refrigerator" Perry or possibly a similar-looking, more contemporary reference, filled the doorway, zipping up his dress pants.

"What's going on, Private?" Brice asked.

Drake held out the receiver. "Got a bad one, sir. It's a Code Yinzer."

Brice's face narrowed. "Oh hell no. That Pittsburgh shit all over again?"

"Only a handful of people know the code, sir. Chances it's a prank are statistically impossible."

Brice grunted and picked up the phone. "Sergeant Brice here. Yes? You don't say. And then what? You did? Wait, and UFOs, too? Well, shit. Pardon my French, Governor." Brice held the receiver to his chest and turned to Drake. "It's a real one, all right."

Drake's face blanched. "What're we gonna do?"

"Get the White House on the line." Brice hung his massive head. "And then pray to whatever God you believe in, and maybe all the ones you don't for good measure."

9:42pm Pacific Standard Time

The ambulance screamed around the corner, lights flashing. Gravity sent two wheels up in the air, the vehicle popped up on the sidewalk, smashing a newspaper kiosk stuffed with utterly-irrelevant headlines to bits. A hardworking sidewalk vendor dived out of the way just in time, scraping his palms on the concrete but otherwise emerging unscathed.

Until he saw the zombie horde shambling down the street, promptly crapped his pants, and ran off in the opposite direction, hands clasped tightly and raised to the sky, uttering a jumbled mash-up of The Lord's Prayer and "Now I Lay Me Down to Sleep."

Inside the ambulance, Elfphonso cursed at the idiot mall Santa who couldn't drive to save his un-life and continued forcing his way down the man's throat.

He'd already broken the Santa's jaw—the man didn't notice, pain receptors were the first things to rot away post-zombification, or *Dawn of the Dead* would've been a hell of a lot shorter—and was shimmying down the tiny tube, elf-bones helpfully squishing to size. The man might not be able to feel him, but he WAS making a lot of weird sounds. Like a cat swallowing the world's biggest hairball. His Adam's apple bulged at Elfphonso's passing, but somehow his throat didn't burst.

Elfphonso hadn't ever been inside a human before—technically, he'd not even met one before he burst out of that shattered snow globe—and wasn't very impressed. Dark, hard to breathe, and very, very slimy.

Somewhere just below the man's sternum, Elfphonso got stuck. He strained against bone and muscle, couldn't push his way past, no matter how hard he tried. Which was just as well because he could smell the bubbling stomach acid just below the tips of his adorably-pointed shoes.

Good enough.

Now he'd effectively tripled in size, able to manipulate all the pulleys and levers of the human world. Thanks to the elf-venom infecting his host's central nervous system, he could use the Santa pretender's muscle memory to turn the steering wheel, goose the gas pedal.

Deliver him to his destiny.

"All shall be Elfphonso!" Elfphonso muttered, lips sliding back and forth against the mall Santa's rubbery trachea. He tried to shake his tiny fist for good measure, but his arms were pretty much pinned at his sides.

His mind, however—

The ambulance roared through an intersection, utterly pancaking an old lady stooped under the weight of several heavy shopping bags, undoubtedly earmarked for some cherub-cheeked grandchildren who'd never be able to listen to "Grandma Got Run Over by a Reindeer" ever again without bursting into tears.

Deep inside the mall Santa, Elfphonso blinked away the image and kept going. He let the vestiges of the man's intellect—if you could call it that—handle the relatively simple task of driving and focused on their destination.

The Whosgotta Christmas Supply Warehouse.

And more specifically, the crate of unshattered snow globes beneath it.

10:06pm Pacific Standard Time

Landfill grunted, working Jimmy's crowbar hard to snap another wooden stave off the life-size sleigh they'd found in all those aisles of Christmatica. "How many more of these do you need?"

Across the warehouse, Jimmy stopped hammering broken pieces of wood across the door long enough to call back, "Five? Six? We gotta do the wind-hos."

"Yeah, okay." She worked the teeth of the crowbar into a slot between boards, then leaned back hard. The wood snapped free, yielding a somewhat battered two-by-four. She leaned down, tossed it in a pile, then went in for another.

Originally their plan had been to get the fuck out of Dodge, but when they went outside JIMMY'S Dodge was out of gas. Landfill didn't let on she knew where the discarded rubber hose and the wet gasoline stain on the pavement came from, and Jimmy barely noticed when she muttered "Fucking Caterpillar," since he was bent over at the knees in another ho-ho-hoing fit.

Semi-bothersome, but he hadn't tried to eat her or fuck her like the other men in the warehouse, so she figured she'd roll with it for the time being.

Given that they had no wheels, and from the reports on TV all hell seemed to be breaking loose across Pine Canyon, they'd decided their next best option was to barricade themselves inside Whosgotta, jury-rig whatever weapons they could, and ride it out until the cops or the Army or a helpful mob of Christmas vigilantes took care of whatever the hell was happening.

Which was why, even though it broke her heart for the second time that night, she was ripping up Santa's whip for spare lumber.

"Door's good," Jimmy said, appearing at her side. "Nobody's getting through that." He scooped up an armful of boards and crossed the warehouse to the first of two windows.

Landfill had to admit, there were worse places to barricade yourself inside.

Even if your boyfriend was dead in the basement.

Tears welled in her eyes, but she choked them back—her feelings weren't going anywhere, any more than Tommy himself was. Time for that later.

Now, she just had to survive Christmas.

A few minutes later, she'd reduced the imitation barn to splintered wood. Jimmy came back, grabbed a fresh armful, and together they boarded up the other window. Then, Jimmy jumped in the forklift and moved some crates in front of the doors, a little extra insurance against a mob of zombie elves (or regular zombies LED by an elf? She didn't know) breaking through.

"Think that's pretty good," Jimmy said, breathing heavily. He sat back down on the forklift and fanned himself.

"Hope so," Landfill said. She felt too anxious to sit down, so leaned against one of the crates instead. "You got anything to drink in this joint?"

"There's a soda machine," Jimmy said, cocking a thumb at the aisle where most of Self-Harm currently resided. "Just take a right at the severed head."

"I was thinking something . . . harder."

Jimmy shook his head. "Put a plug in the jug back in the '90s. Used to hit it pretty heavy, until . . . "

"Until what?"

"Damn near ho-hung myself with a string of Christmas lights. I liked drinking, but I love being alive, so it wasn't much of a contest." Jimmy drummed his fingers on the side of the forklift. "You sure you don't want a soda? Got quarters in my desk. I think."

Landfill shook her head.

"Okay." Jimmy was quiet for a minute, then said, "What's with the Landfill stuff, anyway? You got a pretty name already. Linnea."

Landfill sighed. "That's the problem. You know

how hard it is to get taken seriously as a Christpunk, if you're a woman?"

"Can't say I do."

"Everybody thinks because I'm a chick, I'm just here for the fuzzy sweaters and Turkish Delight. I mean, Caterpillar doesn't even know half as many carols as I do, and the kid legit thinks the lyrics are 'Hark the Harold angel.' Like Rudolph the red-nosed reindeer, here's Hark the Harold angel. What the fuck's a Harold angel?"

Jimmy gestured expansively at the warehouse. "If that was a thing, we'd have it."

"Harold angel my ass." She hopped up on the crate, resting her chin in her hands. "Hope he's okay. The backstabbing little coward."

Jimmy reached over and patted her on the knee. "I'm sure he is. This's all gonna blow over. Soon."

"Maybe."

Jimmy stood, grabbing the crowbar and giving it a little twirl. "You know something?"

"What?"

"Nobody takes me seriously, either. I'm a middle-aged middle manager at a Christmas warehouse. Peaked in my twenties. But the thing is, I'm okay with that. I always figured I'd die here at Whosgotta, someday. Because when it comes down to it, there's only one thing that's ever mattered to me."

Landfill looked up at him. "What's that?"

"Christmas. And we're not gonna let some stupid little elf stop us from seeing another one, are we?"

December 25th, 2019
1:15am Eastern Standard Time

Bianca Glover, the Chief of Staff to the current administration, poked her head into the Oval Office.

The Commander in Chief had his head planted firmly on the Resolute desk. He moaned, lolled from side to side. Knocked over a miniature bust of Grover Cleveland, Glover's personal favorite president. The bust had been an Inauguration Day gift to POTUS.

Back when she still viewed him as strong, decisive, and one of the better lays she'd had in her twenty-two years in Washington.

"[REDACTED]," Glover said softly. "You have to make a decision."

POTUS slowly raised his head. Tears streamed from his eyes, his hair stood up in a cowlick. A little dribble of snot oozed out of his nose.

"It's not fair," the Commander in Chief whined. "Just a couple hours ago, [ALSO REDACTED] and I were lighting the National Christmas Tree. Sipping hot chocolate. Tucking in little [YEP, REDACTED] and [OH YEAH, YOU BETTER BELIEVE THAT ONE'S REDACTED]. It was a p-p-perfect Ch-ch-ristmas!"

Glover fought back the urge to vomit, slap him across the face, or invoke the 25th Amendment. Instead, she ambled into the office, practicing the meditation techniques her Swedish yoga teacher Stretch Armstrong insisted would center her prana and keep her from dropping dead of an embolism, and leaned against the Resolute desk, gently stroking his shoulder.

"Shh," she said, using the same soft tone of voice

she did with Stretch whenever he pulled something. "It's all right."

POTUS choked back tears. "I know, I know, it's just—Yinzers! Hasn't been one since the Johnson administration, and back then they could just blame it on the—"

"Terrorists," Glover said. "There's ALWAYS terrorists. According to the CIA the Baader-Meinhof gang are coming back into vogue."

"Baader-Meinhof? Somebody was just telling me about them the other day."

"See?" Glover ran a hand through his hair, making his heart puh-rum-pum-pum like a little drummer boy. "There's always someone to blame. All YOU have to do is press the button." She frowned. "It's not actually a button. You know what I mean. They did brief you, right?"

POTUS nodded gravely. "It's just—it's Christmas. What would little baby Jesus think?"

"That guy who sings 'My Christmas Dick?' Who gives a shit?"

"No," POTUS said, gesturing at the crucifix on the wall next to a velvet portrait of Elvis drawing a velvet portrait of FDR. "The actual little baby Jesus."

Glover scoffed. "What kind of a president gives a fuck what a baby thinks?" She lowered her face next to his—he wouldn't meet her eyes, just kept staring into the oak timbers of the desk Queen Victoria gave to Rutherford B. Hayes, who you totally learned about in school, dumbass. "Push. The. Button."

He whimpered.

She headed for the door. Paused, one hand on the knob. "If you don't—" and now he actually looked up and met her gaze, and beneath the tears was a look that matched the name of his big-ass desk and made her think maybe she WOULDN'T have to pull the Veep out of his favorite strip club after all (Millard Fuckmore's on M St NW).

So, she said nothing.

Knowing despite his protestations he'd do the right thing: nuke a small American city and blame it on the villain from *Die Hard* or whatever.

1:25am Arctic Time

Thousands of miles to the north, another assistant briefed the Acting Santa on the situation in Pine Canyon.

You know, the one they started.

"Where's Colonel Claus?" the Acting Santa bellowed, because even though he had none of the original St. Nick's marvelous abilities, he DID do a pretty good impression—could make his belly jiggle like ye olde bowlful of jelly, too—and that was how the Clausian Hegemony chose their leaders.

Correct—the most advanced civilization on Earth didn't decide who sat in their big chair based on smarts, gumption, or even which candidate was made from the cum of the leader their parents liked for whatever reason. No, said advanced civilization thought MIMARCHY[1] was the best form of government.

---

[1] Mimarchy (Noun). A monarchy where the leader is chosen via an audition process where a council of learned elders picks the candidate who can best imitate a fictional character.

RETURN OF THE LIVING ELVES

The Assistant, a put-upon half-Claus/half-Kringle with a can-do work ethic and a crippling heroin addiction, toed the carpet. "She's MIA, sir, maybe KIA. We have a report of a sleigh going down over Pine Canyon. Mass casualties. The sleigh was unregistered, but a Naughty Cam outside Bakersfield picked up some images that look like her. And some guy. He was pretty cute actually, I wonder if he's sing—"

"Dammit, Maggie," the Acting Santa pounded his desk. "Send a team to look for survivors." His face narrowed. "And witnesses."

The Assistant shivered, mostly from his early withdrawal symptoms but also because this next part was really fucking scary. "It's not that simple. We've been monitoring human reports, apparently there's a mob of—" he made scare quotes with his fingers, "zombies led by an—" scare quotes again, "*elf*. We're assuming the sleigh's propellant aerosolized and is causing mass hallucinations."

"Mass hallu—"

Another Assistant stuck her head in the door. "Piotr Cottontailovna's on line 2. Sounds pissed, something about a zombie attack?"

The Acting Santa stared daggers at the first Assistant. "Tell him I'm indisposed. And shut the door."

Assistant 2 shut the door, then almost as quickly opened it again. "Umm, we've got Colonel Quataffy on line 3. And, uh, the acting President of Pieanmar. What's—Lady Incisa, a couple talking horses, the Lord of Gourds, uh—Lucky O'Bragh is VERY concerned about allegations of elf abuse—"

"Deal with it."

The second assistant gulped and shut the door again.

The Acting Santa slowly rose from his desk to stand at the window, gazing out across the towering spires of Clausington, the sensible ranch-style homes of Peppermint Park, the disgusting, shit-smeared hovels of Elf Town. "My god, after all these years." He balled up a fist. "Red Maggie, you stupid, conceited, hubristic, connivingly evil—"

"What's wrong?" the Assistant asked. "My models still show—"

The Acting Santa held up a hand to silence him. "You've never heard of the Elf Improvement Project, have you?"

The Assistant shook his head.

"Of course not, you'd have sold the info for a fix."

"What? I would never—"

"Come on, you can't lie to another junkie. We all do heroin up here. It's the only thing TO do."

"Oh."

The Acting Santa returned to his desk, slid out a drawer. He carefully laid a pair of syringes, a spoon, a rubber hose, and all the other glorious accouterments of intravenous drug use on the desk.

"First, we're going to get high as fuck," the Acting Santa said.

"And then?" the Assistant asked, hopping back and forth like a child on Christmas morning.

"Send Neil to the store for cigarettes. And THEN we're going to call in a White Christmas."

The Assistant bobbed his head up and down, the implication of nuclear annihilation going in one heroin-addicted ear and out the other. "Sweet."

RETURN OF THE LIVING ELVES

They shot up, waited for Neil to get back from the store with a pack of smokes, and then the Acting Santa gave the mellowest mass-murder order in history.

"Are you high right now?" the Lieutenant Colonel on the other end asked. "Wait, I don't care. One White Christmas, coming right up!"

```
December 24th, 2019 (again)
10:46pm Pacific Standard Time
```

He was in hell.

Matt Kringle made his way through the deliriously demented streets of Pine Canyon, memories of Lollipopland atrocities superimposed over every new, horrific sight. Was that a middle-aged deacon eating the entrails of a Salvation Army volunteer, or a bubblegum bison grazing on a field of sugared glass?

He didn't know.

Didn't care.

Ran from cover to cover, killing when he had to, the sharp retort of his K-22 pistol ringing in his ears, gun smoke mercifully crowding out far worse scents.

The zombies were everywhere.

Snarling, slavering, hunting. Feeding. He passed an overturned minivan, oil leaking onto the pavement like Red Maggie's blood, the occupants unrecognizable hunks of gnawed flesh. A Catholic Church, Our Lady of Who Gives a Shit, the doors battered down, a benediction of screams echoing from the vestibule. A lowly bar, beacon for those with no one else on Christmas Eve, the painted windows shattered, a shadow play of fire and torment conducted by the writhing shapes within.

At each, he set his jaw, and looked no harder than he had to, to ensure no one was coming for him. All he had was a gun and a burning desire to see this thing through to the bitter end.

Whatever that might be.

Change everything.

Maybe another Claus lie. But he didn't think so. The story Red Maggie spun made an awful lot of sense. In the absence of a natural-born Santa, something unseen in the Polar world in centuries, the Clausian Hegemony thought outside the box. Exhumed the body of the original St. Nicholas, long-interred in an undisclosed location beneath humble Peppermint Park.

Home of the Kringles, the second-class citizens.

The Clausian scientists took DNA samples. Worked their scientific wizardry, combining everything that made the first St. Nick himself with a retrovirus. Tucked it all away in a fruitcake so no one would eat it.

Of course, every son of a stocking on the Council wanted to be THE ONE, but Red Maggie—to her credit—wasn't having it. Maybe she was the worst of them, but she also owned it. Knew what she was, and more importantly what the other Clauses were. None of them were worthy, not a single one.

So, she hid the fruitcake away, with her other mistakes.

Typical Clausian idiocy lost all of it.

She'd been too far gone to tell him everything, just the broad strokes, but Kringle had spent enough time around Clauses to fill the rest in for himself.

Upshot was, he could fix everything.

Find the fruitcake, save the world.

If he survived.

He entered an industrial park—the Christmas supply warehouse where Elfphonso got free couldn't be far. If he was lucky, the fruitcake would be there too.

Long as he could force himself to eat the thing, there was hope.

One thing there wasn't, was cover. Kringle abandoned stealth for speed, jogged through a parking lot empty of cars, the various businesses—mostly unremarkable collections of letters—gone dark for the holiday.

One still had the lights on, something called Kaltenbreuer's. He thought about stopping in to quaff whatever the human equivalent of sugarplum schnapps was, steady his nerves a bit—he'd not been on a mission in years, and Red Maggie's death had affected him in bizarre ways he hadn't expected and couldn't even articulate—but despite the lights they looked closed, nobody inside.

And besides, saving the world couldn't wait, could it?

Kringle passed the entrance, double-timing it, when the door banged open. He whirled, expected to see a drunk human—and reconsidering the possibility of maybe-sort-of stopping for a beverage—but a dark shape lunged at him. The impact bowled him over and he fell hard on the asphalt, cracking the back of his head.

Claws raked his face, hot slashes opening up his

cheeks. He lashed out blindly, head fuzzed. Connected with something, felt a heavy weight lift off his abdomen.

Kringle rolled right, popped back up to his feet, muscle memory carrying him through.

His attacker—a woman, or something that used to be a woman, because her skin was green and her yawning jaws revealed far more teeth than she should've had per his long-ago Human Biology 101 class—hissed at him, swiped the air with her claws.

Kringle pulled his pistol, but by the time he leveled it she was on him again, slamming her body into his. They crashed into the brick wall behind him, he squeezed the trigger, pumping bullets into her body point-blank.

She jerked, writhed, pulsated.

And bit down.

Her four rows of teeth took a hunk out of his trapezoid. Kringle screamed, knocked her away with a backhand while simultaneously bringing his pistol to bear.

A squeeze of the trigger, and her brains blew right the fuck out the back of her skull.

The body jerked, slid down the wall to crumple at his feet. Her jaws spasmed, bits of his flesh still stuck in all those teeth.

Then stilled.

Kringle probed the wound, gritting his teeth against the pain. Not deep, no.

But enough.

He tore a strip off his shirt, bound his new wound as best he could, then raced down the street.

Praying he'd find the fruitcake in time.

RETURN OF THE LIVING ELVES

December 24th/25th, 2019
11:52pm   Rocky   Mountain   Standard
   Time/1:52am Arctic Time

Several time zones and 3500 miles apart, two phones rang.

Receivers were lifted, grim commands received. No one asked for clarification.

They were way past that.

In two separate bunkers, keys were turned. Prayers uttered. Workaday stiffs cursed their goddamn luck at drawing the worst possible shift they could.

But in the end, they pushed the button, because that was their goddamn job.

Several time zones and 3500 miles apart, two missiles launched.

Heading for the tiny town of Pine Grove.

11:07pm Pacific Standard Time

Jimmy swayed, trying not to fall over. The girl on his shoulders was heavier than she looked. Or he was weaker than he thought, which was a distinct possibility he didn't much care for. "You see anything?"

He was playing human stepping stool so Landfill could look out the cracks of the boarded-up windows, see what the hell was going on outside.

Because it sounded like the world's biggest Christmas parade just crash-landed in their parking lot. Ambulance sirens, screeching tires. He would've thought it was the authorities, but when he heard a couple hundred dull, dead voices singing, "Fa la la la la la" over and over again?

He damn near dropped some coal in his stocking.

"Yes?" Landfill replied.

"Care to elab-ho-rate?" Jimmy asked. "Or you want to boost me up there next?"

Landfill hopped down off his shoulders. "So, uh, bad news. There's a whole crowd of people converging on the parking lot, walking like they're in a Romero movie."

"Onward, my legions!" a mechanically-amplified voice hissed. "Batter down the doors! We shall first conquer this Christmas supply warehouse, and then the world!"

"Guess he figured out how to use the ambulance's PA," Landfill said. "That's your elf buddy, I'm assuming?"

Jimmy nodded.

"Good," Landfill said, clutching the hammer Jimmy'd used to board up the doors and windows. "Then I can make him pay for what he did to Tommy. This is all his fault."

"Yep, sure is." Jimmy was impressed with her resolve. A small part of him felt pretty bad about lying to her, and if she'd asked a bunch of specific questions, he was worried his face would give him away, but she didn't. "Let's ho-ho-hope he makes himself pay out there in the parking lot."

Landfill snarled and stalked away, taking a few practice swings with the hammer.

Jimmy picked his own crowbar back up but didn't bother doing the same. He wasn't planning on fighting anybody. Based on what Landfill had said, if their barricades failed, they'd be overwhelmed in seconds.

The thought sent a shiver down his spine. One thing he'd always been deathly afraid of was having a bunch of old people eat him alive. Not as afraid as he was of getting sap all over him, then having Lorna's cat rub itself up and down his body until some asshole hunter mistook him for a sasquatch, but still.

Pretty scary.

They could move down to the basement, get a few more layers of security between them and the mob outside, but then they'd be trapped, plus the kid's body was down there, and he didn't want to make Landfill look at THAT, especially because then she might start asking all those questions about how exactly the kid's brains ended up all over the floor.

A noise at the back door on the other side of the warehouse caught his attention. He'd boarded it up like the others, even though he'd almost forgot it was there. They never used it for nothing because it was just an emergency exit, and this was the first emergency they'd ever had.

Jimmy cocked his ear—

WHAM! WHAM! WHAM!

Sounded like somebody was kicking the door. Which was really fucking rude, considering all the trouble they'd gone to to board it up in the first place.

"Landfill!" he yelled, breaking into something that resembled a light jog. "They're at the back door!"

He didn't know if she knew where the back door was, but hoped she'd follow the sound of his voice. If the zombies broke through, one could brain 'em while the other tacked boards back up.

Jimmy nearly tripped over a fallen Christmas tree—fake, so no sap to worry about—and rounded the aisle. The back door with the big red EMERGENCY sign lay just beyond.

Something crashed into it from the other side.

Jimmy approached, clutching the crowbar tightly. The boards were holding, for now, but if—

BLAM!

A hole erupted in the door, a bullet whizzed by Jimmy's ear.

"Ho-ly shit!" he cried, throwing himself to the floor.

"Who's shooting?" Landfill called from the next aisle. "Cops?"

"God, I hope so," Jimmy said, jamming his hands over his ears just as another barrage of shots ripped through the door.

He chanced a quick glance. The shots had formed one big hole in the middle of the door. A large hand reached through, feeling for the doorknob, then brushed up against one of the boards.

"Dammit," a voice called from the other side. The hand retracted, then was replaced by a square-jawed, dirt-and-blood streaked face. "Anybody home?"

Jimmy shot a cautious glance at Landfill, who was creeping along the wall. She shrugged—*nobody I know*.

"You with them?" Jimmy asked.

"With who?"

"The Salvation Army! No, the fucking mob of zombies out front, the hell do you think I mean?"

The face winced. "No, I'm not with them."

"Then who ARE you?" Landfill called.

The face blinked, apparently surprised at the other voice. "My name's—SERGEANT Matt Kringle. And you've got to let me inside, right now."

Jimmy shot another glance at Landfill. "Sergeant? They finally called out the National Guard. Where's the rest of your, uh, platoon?"

"I'm alone," Kringle said. "Look, I need you to open the door right—"

A chorus of dull fa-la-las echoed from the other side of the door.

"Hold on."

BLAM BLAM BLAM!

"Just a couple strays," Kringle said. "The main group are bunched up in the parking lot. Now, you going to let me in or what?"

Jimmy scratched his chin, or tried, his fingers got caught in the brand-new beard. "How do I know you're not one of them?"

"You just heard me drop three of the bastards. So?"

"Jimmy," Landfill said quietly. "Maybe he can help us."

Maybe he could. Or maybe this was some trick. Still—

WHAM!

Something slammed into the roll-up door on the other side of the warehouse. Luckily, the big rig was still blocking the loading dock, so it must've been

BRIAN ASMAN

bodies, not the ambulance wielded as a battering ram. Thankfully—otherwise their barricades would be about as useful as a tarp in a hurricane.

"Okay," Jimmy said, getting to his feet. "One sec."

"Thanks," Kringle replied. "I'll just—oh, for the love of Christmas!"

Another barrage of gunshots erupted outside the door. Luckily no stray rounds punched through the wood, so Jimmy hopped to his feet and yanked off a couple boards with the crowbar. Landfill joined him, working the teeth of her hammer and ripping out nails. In seconds they'd cleared the boards and yanked the door open.

The guy standing there was big. Broad-shouldered. Corded muscle rippling down both arms. If the National Guard could only send one guy, Jimmy thought, at least they tapped Rambo.

Then Jimmy noticed his bloody-yet-Christmas-patterned BDUs and wondered if maybe he was hallucinating again.

Kringle pushed past them into the warehouse. Jimmy caught a glimpse of his ears—oddly pointed—and kept the crowbar low at his side, just in case.

"Where is it?" Kringle asked, breathing heavily.

"Where's what?" Jimmy replied.

"The fruitcake."

Jimmy cocked his chin at Landfill. "He talking about your buddy Suicidal Tendency?"

"Self-HARM," Landfill stressed.

"No," Kringle said, shaking his head. "An actual fruitcake. You seen it anywhere?"

Jimmy blinked. "Uh, a FRUITCAKE fruitcake? Ho. I mean, no."

Kringle turned, looked him up and down. He

stepped back and crossed his arms over his chest. "You ate it, didn't you?"

Jimmy gulped. "No?"

"I don't know what this fruitcake shit is, but we should really barricade the door again," Landfill said.

"Yeah, okay."

The three of them worked quickly, securing the door in minutes.

Across the warehouse, the sounds of slams and whams and the stupid little Elf screeching at his minions continued.

"All right," Kringle said, something heavy in his voice. "This isn't ideal, but it'll have to—" A large, blocky device on his wrist beeped. Kringle glanced at it, pressed a couple buttons, then his face fell. "Shit."

"What is it?" Landfill asked.

"We don't have much time. Those Claus sons of bitches called in a White Christmas, just like Red Maggie said they would."

Jimmy frowned. "We never get no snow here."

"It's a euphemism," Kringle said.

"For what?"

"Nuclear annihilation."

"Fuck," Landfill muttered.

Jimmy's heart thumped. All this elf shit, and now an A-bomb to boot? The hits were coming so fast and furious he barely had time to wonder who the hell Red Maggie was, or—did the Sergeant actually say *those* Claus *sons of bitches?*

And what kind of a name was Kringle, anyway?

"The humans are probably launching nukes of their own," Kringle said. "Same thing they did in Louisville back in the '80s."

"Humans?" Jimmy said.

"Nobody nuked Louisville," Landfill added.

"Not ALL of it," Kringle replied. "Now look, I'm not going to sugarcoat things. If the zombies don't get us first, the bombs will. We've got one chance. Jimmy, you really ate that fruitcake? Be honest."

Jimmy stared at his feet. "I got diabetes. My blood sugar—"

"Fine." Kringle reached into his pocket and pulled out something that looked like a flashlight.

"What's that do?" Landfill asked.

Kringle pressed a button on the side. "This."

11:14pm Pacific Standard Time

Elfphonso—deep inside the ooey-gooey insides of the dead-yet-elf-animated Mall Santa—sized up the situation and scowled.

With both the Mall Santa's face and his own.

When he'd ordered his horde to shamble towards the warehouse, he assumed the fat and cowardly warehouse manager was still stuck in a locked room in the basement, alongside the young man he'd nipped on the ankle, who would've surely turned him by now. Never in his elfiest dreams did he imagine said warehouse manager would've summoned up his courage and BARRICADED himself inside.

Elfphonso could almost hear his brethren calling to him from deep within their individual snow globes. He had to free them, otherwise this entire escapade would be for naught. He'd mustered an impressive army, but to take the Pole itself, he'd need millions more conscripts. And the only way to get them would be to unleash those like him, let them pour over these strange Southerlands, converting the entire populace into a war machine the likes of which the world had never seen.

The Clauses wouldn't know what hit them. IF he could get inside.

A burly man in a Rams jersey got a running start and launched himself head-first into the rollup door. The metal wailed like a guitar solo, the man went stumbling back, blood pouring from his head.

He set his jaw and tried again, and again, until he collapsed on the loading dock, his brains leaking out a ragged wet crease atop his skull.

Elfphonso shook the Mall Santa's head. What a waste.

No amount of zombie power would get them inside. They needed a battering ram.

With a makeshift ramp to clear the loading dock, the ambulance would work perfectly, if only the cursed big rig wasn't in the way. The rig itself was way too heavy, would've required the construction of an actual ramp, and he had neither time nor materials to accomplish such a task.

"Think!" Elfphonso implored the Mall Santa.

A long silence ensued from his body-mate, enough to make Elfphonso wonder if his venom had rotted the man's brain cells, before finally a stray thought came back, sizzling down the man's spine.

Maybe the keys are in it?

Shit.

Manipulating arms and legs, Elfphonso tottered over to the truck and hefted himself inside. The interior stank of old fast food and infrequent showers. A St. Christopher medal was pinned to the sun visor.

Elfphonso took a moment to reflect on the sweet, sweet joy he'd experienced when he turned the truck driver, then started rooting around in the cab. He tossed a Big Gulp cup over his shoulder, brushed porno mags off the passenger seat, and finally—with the prompting of whatever remained of the Mall Santa's brain—checked the ignition.

Bingo!

Elfphonso asked a quick question of the Mall Santa, received an equally quick response. No, he had no idea how to drive a big rig.

But maybe someone else did.

Leaning out the door, Elfphonso shouted at his minions, "Do any of you know how to drive this thing?"

The horde stopped their various, ineffectual attempts to punch or kick or head-butt down the door and looked at him.

An elderly woman raised her hand.

"Good," Elfphonso said, and within minutes the truck was backed into a parking spot a good distance from the loading dock.

He returned to the ambulance, fired up the engine. There was still one problem. The loading dock was a good four feet high.

"Minions!" Elfphonso called, snapping the Mall Santa's fingers. "Ramp, please."

One by one, dozens of zombie shoppers

formed a human pyramid at the base of the loading dock.

Elfphonso grinned with the Mall Santa's mouth and gunned the engine.

∞ Nonstandard Supradimensional Time

Stars exploded in Jimmy's eyes, the room went black, his consciousness catapulting out of his skull, past the spiders crawling on the ceiling and into the night sky, screaming towards a mass of pulsating, fluctuating lights.

Aurora borealis.

Sucking him in, subsuming the middle-aged diabetic warehouse foreman with bad knees. For a glimmering instant, Jimmy was pure light and pure joy and pure fucking goodness, simultaneously surrounded by and exploding with the sort of love a human can't even begin to conceptualize, let alone understand or describe.

In the smallest fraction of microsecond, and even half of that again, Jimmy's soul snapped like an old rubber band.

And then was squirted out, primordial Jimmy-juice splurting across time and space and several dimensions currently unknown to science, into the brains of every person who'd ever donned a furry red hat and hollered HO HO HO at anybody who'd listen.

For one infinite instant, a mundane Christmas

supply warehouse manager became one with every Santa Claus who'd ever been, or ever would be.

Most were fakes—department store Santas, schlubby middle managers donning a hat at the office Christmas party, even a couple actors playing the big man in Hollywood movies, everybody from Edmund Gwenn to Tim Allen (who were both coincidentally HIGH AS FUCK ON COCAINE during their respective performances).

But Jimmy?

Jimmy learned something that would have made him the envy of every ten-year-old, every kid straddling the fence between childhood and adult bullshit, half-suspecting Santa was a lie but too terrified to utter the thought out loud, lest they be jinxed, end up with a stocking full of coal instead of the Yuletide razzmatazz they've been halfheartedly working towards all year by choosing to be slightly less shitty on certain select occasions.

Santa was REAL. Not a story, not a metaphor. FUCKING REAL.

But not a person, either. A position. An office. The supreme and autocratic ruler of an entire subculture. Lord of the North. Dictator of Christmasland. Signer of the Imagination Accords, Commander-in-Chief of the Krampus Corps. Master of Elfkind.

The Santa Claus.

Jimmy saw it all, from Santa Khan onwards. The separation of his descendants into Clauses and Kringles. The succession wars, the anti-Santas, the ill-advised incursions into Lollipopland. Blood and fire and genocide, all while children the world over left out milk and cookies, opened presents, whispered prayers to their one true God, the one who shared a holiday with the Nazarene but outclassed him in omniscience and omnipotence.

As quickly as it left, Jimmy's fractured consciousness slammed back into his body.

"It's real!" he cried. "Christmas is REAL!"

Landfill was at his side, steadying him. Drool ran down his chin. He leaned on her for a moment, then righted himself.

Trembling with all the power of motherfucking SANTA CLAUS HIMSELF, BITCHES.

Ho, ho, ho.

11:22am Pacific Standard Time

Landfill gaped at Jimmy. He looked different. He was still wearing his ridiculous heart-covered boxers, but his cheeks had a rosy red glow, he stood up straight, somehow he'd acquired a pair of tiny spectacles during his out of body experience.

Most importantly, a Santa hat now sat on his head, crimson and gleaming.

Or more accurately, if she looked closely—and she really wished she hadn't—his head had BECOME a Santa hat. The line of demarcation between forehead and furry white band was fuzzy, at best.

"Ew."

"My god, it worked!" Kringle cried. "It—argh—worked!" He collapsed to his knees, gripping the side of his neck.

Which, Landfill now realized, was covered with a blood-leaking makeshift bandage.

And had his skin taken on something of a greenish pallor?

"What's wrong, son?" Santa-Jimmy asked.

Kringle gestured vaguely towards the parking lot. "On the way here. One of 'em . . . got the jump on me. Ack!"

"And you CAME IN here?" Landfill shouted, casually taking up a position behind Kringle. She lifted the hammer, aiming at the back of his skull.

"I had no choice!" Kringle cried.

"Wait!" Santa-Jimmy called, holding up a hand.

Landfill took a step back, but stayed ready to bash the Army guy's brains in.

Santa-Jimmy looked around quickly, then settled on the seat of the forklift. He patted his lap. "Come here, little boy."

Kringle looked up, sweat coursing down his face. "What?"

"Yeah, I don't know, but maybe just do it?" Landfill said.

"Argh . . . okay. Help me?"

"Uh-uh, I've had way too many zombie dudes get fresh with me today." Landfill bit her lip. "Or rotten, really."

"No time for jokes, little girl," Santa-Jimmy said, and ordinarily she would've found that patronizing as fuck, but since Santa was apparently real and a warehouse manager, she let it slide.

Kringle struggled to his feet, loped across the floor, nearly falling, but managed to settle into Santa-Jimmy's lap. It looked completely ridiculous, the man with the action-figure body sitting astride Santa's knee like a child, but Landfill had made her peace with ridiculousness a long time ago, along with several other shitty MTV reality shows from the mid-00s.

"What do you want for Christmas, little boy?" Santa-Jimmy asked. "More than anything in the world."

Kringle's head lolled, his mouth yawned open—two extra rows of pointy teeth were pushing through his gums. "Seriously?"

"Just fucking say it, will you?" Santa-Jimmy made a hurry-up motion.

"I want to not be a . . . zombie."

"And have you been a good boy this year?"

Kringle was silent for way too long.

"Screw it," Santa-Jimmy said. "I'm the goddamn Santa and I make the rules. Uh, I just need a—" he looked around the warehouse furiously, "Landfill! Get me a present!"

"A present?"

Santa-Jimmy nodded. "Any present. Just something he can open."

"Yeah, okay." Landfill rushed into the warehouse. More crashes and smashes and butchered Christmas carols erupted from the front, but she didn't have time to worry about that. She ran down one aisle—nothing but stupid snowmen. Checked the next, a bunch of trees. Manger scenes, a life-size camel, wreath after fucking wreath.

Until, near the front of the warehouse, she finally found it.

A big novelty present, wrapped in red and yellow paper, tied with a bow.

She picked it up—empty, thankfully—and pivoted to run back to Jimmy.

That's when the ambulance crashed through the roll-up door.

```
11:33pm Pacific Standard Time
```

"Little help!" Santa-Jimmy yelled, trying his level best to keep the snarling zombie Army guy at bay. Kringle's jaws snapped uncomfortably close to his neck. Santa-Jimmy pushed him away, grabbed him by the throat, and slammed him on the ground, using his Yuletide bulk to keep the man from moving.

Too much.

The sound of rending metal and screeching tires erupted from the other side of the warehouse. Landfill ran towards them, carrying a present almost as big as she was.

Kringle head-butted Santa-Jimmy, which hurt like a bastard, but he slammed the man's head against the concrete floor with a solid THWACK.

That seemed to settle him.

For the moment.

Blood gushed from Santa-Jimmy's nose, but it barely registered. He just focused on controlling the ravenous elf-zombie.

"What should I do with this?" Landfill asked.

"Open it!" Santa-Jimmy cried.

"Really?"

"He can't," Santa-Jimmy cocked his bloody chin

at Kringle. "If you open it, it'll work. I hope."

Landfill set the present down and tore into it, ripping wrapping paper with a sharp crackle.

Fa-la-las rose from the other side of the warehouse.

Santa-Jimmy chanced a glance, more elf-zombies were shambolically stumbling over assorted Christmas odds and ends. He didn't see the elf, but that little fuck had to be around, somewhere.

Landfill finished opening the present, extended an empty box in Santa-Jimmy's direction. "So?"

"There!" Santa-Jimmy said. "Just what you wanted."

Kringle spasmed, tossed Jimmy aside with preternatural strength, and lunged, four rows of teeth a-snapping.

Santa-Jimmy closed his eyes, preparing for the worst.

And then—

A Christmas miracle.

"What . . . happened?" Kringle groaned.

Santa-Jimmy looked up. Kringle was standing over him, wavering like a punch-drunk boxer, a faraway look in his eyes.

But a PINK tint to his skin.

Kringle coughed, a dozen teeth fell from his mouth and clattered on the floor. "Damn. I feel like shi—"

The other elf-zombies rounded the aisle, a mismatched battalion of human beings from every walk of life. All fa-la-laing and snapping their teeth.

"No time!" Santa-Jimmy bellowed, jumping to his feet. "You still got that hand cannon?"

Kringle swallowed, then nodded, snapping a fresh

clip into his pistol. The elf-zombies were mere yards away.

"White Christmas," Kringle said. "We've got to stop it."

"How?" Landfill asked.

"We need . . . a sleigh."

Santa-Jimmy shot a glance at the boards barricading the back door. "Uh, yeah. Kinda cannibalized our last one to keep these guys out."

Kringle sighted down his pistol, blasted an elf-zombie in the middle of the forehead. He dropped, the others kept coming.

"Onward, my minions!" a high-pitched voice screeched.

"Least we know where the elf went," Santa-Jimmy muttered.

"Think!" Kringle cried, pumping bullets into the oncoming horde. "This is a goddamn Christmas supply warehouse, you don't have anything else?"

Santa-Jimmy scratched his chin, going over his mental inventory. Manger scenes, they had a ton. Individual reindeer? You betcha. But sleighs? Surprisingly rare.

Except—

"There's one in the basement," Santa-Jimmy said. "But it's . . . uh . . . unorthodox."

"Doesn't matter," Kringle replied. "Get it up to the roof."

"How're we going to do that?"

"Fuck if I know, you're the Santa. Christmas miracles are kinda your thing."

"Fair enough." Santa-Jimmy turned to Landfill. "C'mon. It's plastic, but I'm gonna need a hand."

"Okay," Landfill said, as Kringle wasted another couple elf-zombies.

```
11:38pm Pacific Standard Time
```

Landfill couldn't help herself from feeling a strange sort of awe—while the upstairs itself was a cornucopia of Christmassy delights, the basement was something else altogether.

For someone who'd never quite felt like she fit in, even with the Christpunks, the sight of all the off-kilter holiday paraphernalia took her breath away.

So taken was she by the Yuletide oddities, she never once thought about the half-open door at the back of the room, nor the stink of blood and assorted bodily fluids emanating from within.

"This'll have to work," Santa-Jimmy said, clapping a hand on a plastic sleigh. Surprisingly, it did not break, which was a very good sign for both our heroes, and the greater Pine Canyon metro area, which had no idea how close it was to being immolated by two different ICBMs launched by two different civilizations.

Landfill gaped at the sleigh. "Are those—?"

"Don't ask," Santa-Jimmy said, slinging a leather-clad, ball-gagged reindeer over his shoulder. "Now c'mon."

Landfill grabbed a couple reindeer under each arm and headed for the stairs.

BLAM! BLAM!

Click,

The basement door crashed open. A thin man in his forties fell down the steps, bouncing ass over ankles until he reached the bottom.

Landfill dropped the reindeer, snagged the hammer from her belt loop.

Didn't wait for the man to right himself, just smashed him on the top of the head. The vibration rocketed up her arm, but he dropped. She banged him on the noggin a couple more times and then he stopped moving.

"Nice work," Santa-Jimmy called.

"Thanks," Landfill said. "Now, how're we gonna get these reindeer up to the roof? Not to mention the sleigh?"

"Same way I do everything," Santa-Jimmy said, cracking his knuckles. "I get my employees to do it for me."

"What—"

Santa-Jimmy closed his eyes for a moment, then snapped his fingers.

A rustling sound arose from the room at the back of the basement.

Landfill gulped. "Wait, what are you—"

"Might want to take those two reindeer upstairs," Santa-Jimmy said. "Don't think you want to see what's next."

RETURN OF THE LIVING ELVES

11:41pm Pacific Standard Time

Kringle was surrounded.

He'd emptied his last clip minutes before, and they just kept coming. Some of them had clearly been through some shit already, one half-zombie drug himself along the floor with tire treads imprinted across his malformed head, trailing a lump of glistening viscera behind him, while another lost both her arms and couldn't do much more than aim a head-butt in his direction.

He snapped her neck and kept moving.

Slow and disorganized, they made for relatively easy targets. Numbers were their one advantage.

Good thing SERGEANT Matt Kringle—he'd promoted himself, in his head, because there wasn't a son-of-a-bitching Claus around to tell him any different—had a bunch of advantages of his own. Strength, speed, extensive black ops combat training—

Plus, he'd recently BEEN a zombie, and knew how shitty it was. He could think like them. Anticipate their every move. Which, to be honest, was mostly wobbling around and trying to bite him, Santa Tzu they most definitely were not.

But still.

Some guy with an exposed, half-chewed penis and a nametag that said STANLEY lunged at him. Kringle stepped aside, slammed his Claus-Bar combat knife into the back of the fucker's skull, and ripped it free, blood spraying a sweatshirted soccer mom with a short brown bob. He dispatched her, too, slammed a shoulder into one of the metal racks, sending it careening over onto another cluster of walking elf-dead.

SPLAT.

He could spend all day slaughtering zombies, but with the incoming heavy ordnance, he needed to wrap things up pronto. As he pirouetted through the warehouse, splashing the walls with blood and decking the halls with intestines, he searched every nook and cranny for their leader.

Elfphonso.

If he killed the alpha elf, he'd still have a stockingful of zombies to contend with, but at least they'd be rudderless, and maybe some of them would get bored and wander off. As a Pole-dwelling Kringle, he'd never seen any zombie movies, not *Night of the Living Dead,* nor *28 Days Later,* or even Lucio Fulci's 1980 masterpiece *Zombie,* so he had no frame of reference for how zombies were supposed to work.

Which was fine, because this was all pretty obvious. Shoot/stab/squash, etc. Even an elf could do it.

(Non-zombie category).

"Get him!" a shrill, elfy voice shrieked.

Kringle slashed through another wave, trying to locate the sound. Where was he? Perched on one of the shelves? Riding on the shoulders of some beefy former stock clerk or tucked in the purse of one of the soccer moms? Clinging to the steel beams strafing the roof of the warehouse?

He kicked another zombie in the head, sent him crashing into a pile of candy canes. Surveyed the oncoming hoard, looking for any clue as to where Elfphonso—

Santa.

Not THE Santa, of course, he was downstairs looking for a sleigh, but there was A Santa, a MALL Santa, a portly man with his broken jaw hanging loose on his face, a glazed look in his eyes, hanging at the back of the mob.

Pointing.

"He's one man!" the elf-voice shouted, and the sound was coming from the Mall Santa's mouth, even though it didn't move.

"What the—" Kringle muttered, wondering if maybe the elf was tucked inside the man's suit, strapped to his chest with a Baby Bjorn—then rolled away, dodging gnashing zombie teeth.

Landfill emerged from the basement, dragging two plastic reindeer under either arm. A few zombies shuffled in her direction.

Kringle needed to buy some time. He dashed straight through the horde, hoping his Christmas miracle would hold long enough for him to get to the Mall Santa. He ducked under the outstretched arms of a high schooler in a letterman jacket, kicked out the knees of an elderly woman, and pushed a few bloated, moaning bodies aside.

The Mall Santa—or the elf hiding inside him—saw Kringle coming, turned, and ran.

"Gotcha," Kringle hissed, giving chase.

"Help meeee!" the Mall Santa screeched. The handful of zombies who'd taken an interest in Landfill whipped their heads around, jaws snapping hungrily.

Kringle chased the Mall Santa through the aisles. The man's arms bobbed rapidly, his cap fell from his head, revealing not long, snowy-down hair but a nearly-bald pate. He careened off a storage rack, rounded the aisle.

Heading for the ambulance, and the relative safety it promised.

Kringle pivoted, running down the next aisle to cut him off—

Something heavy slammed into him, knocking him to the ground.

Followed by a deluge of zombie bulk, landing on him, crushing the breath from his lungs.

Until they blocked out the fluorescent lights buzzing on the ceiling, high above.

`11:46pm Pacific Standard Time`

The minute she reached the top of the basement steps, Landfill froze, a gimp reindeer under either arm, cowed by the chaos.

The thick stench of blood—undercut with gingerbread—hung thick in the air. Slaughtered zombies lay everywhere, gaping wounds in their heads, stomachs ripped open, intestines fanning out on the concrete like moist, shit-filled garlands.

A handful of non-slaughtered zombies heard the door open and shambled in her direction.

"Shit!" Landfill said, calling back over her shoulder, "Where am I taking these things?"

Santa-Jimmy grunted from somewhere down in the dark, then said, "There's a door near my office. It goes to another storage room, there's a ladder up to the roof."

"Lotta storage rooms in this place."

"Almost like it's a warehouse."

A shrill sound that might've been some sort of command erupted from behind the main mass of zombies. The couple heading in her direction abruptly turned, heading towards the front of the warehouse with all the urgency of the teenaged food court employees they'd been in life.

Landfill shrugged and hurried to the office. The door next to Jimmy's was unlocked, thankfully. She pushed it open, found a relatively empty space except for some cases of soda that went into the machine Santa-Jimmy kept talking about.

And a metal ladder, going up to a hatch in the roof.

Landfill dropped one reindeer, held the other awkwardly, and climbed up the ladder. It took a minute, but she made it, trying her level best to ignore all the horrific, ambient zombie-noise emanating from the warehouse, and found the Masterlock for the trap door thankfully hanging open. She removed the lock, letting it CLANG to the warehouse floor, and pushed through onto the roof.

Stars sparkled in the night sky above. For a moment she relished the near-calm, the soft breeze, the fires burning in the distance—

Oh, shit.

Landfill set the reindeer down, turned to head back down the ladder to get the other. The storage room door opened, and Santa-Jimmy pushed through butt-first, lugging a plastic sleigh. It wasn't nearly as big as the one they'd destroyed to barricade the warehouse, but if he sucked his belly in, Santa-Jimmy could maybe squeeze into it.

And hopefully the thing wouldn't immediately collapse.

Santa-Jimmy paused at the base of the ladder, looking up at Landfill and the aperture in the roof, back down at the sleigh. He frowned, scratching his well-bearded chin.

"Uh, think we got a problem."

"It won't fit?" Landfill replied, feeling dumb, because of course that's what he meant.

But her brief mental self-flagellation was interrupted when another shape shuffled through the door—tall and wiry, the kind of build that made her weak in the knees. The silhouette looked exactly like—

"Tommy!"

Santa-Jimmy's eyes went wide. "Whoa, no, no no no, you don't want to look at—"

Landfill was already coming down the ladder, the gimp reindeer left lonely on its side on the roof. She nearly slipped off the rungs in her haste, dropped the last five feet, landing like a ninja and rushing past a startled Jimmy to—

"Oh god!" Landfill cried, backpedaling.

She'd thought wrong, this wasn't her dearest Tommy at all. He had the build, and most of the greasepaint, and that WAS Tommy's shirt, wasn't it?

But the face . . .

Dear god, the FACE.

Half of his face was gone, lost in a thick crust of blood. A fold of skin flapped open at his skull, revealing chipped bone, dried cerebral fluid.

Landfill gagged and sobbed at the same time, a

hand going to her mouth, bile burning hot in the back of her throat.

"Nooo!" she screamed, then puked all over Zombie-Tommy's boots.

11:49pm Pacific Standard Time

Santa-Jimmy jumped back, dodging rancid bile. Landfill was bent over at the waist, gagging, while Zombie-Tommy seemed practically stoic, just standing there—more like the voodoo zombies of old than ravenous Romero creations—awaiting his next order.

"Sorry," Santa-Jimmy mumbled. "It seemed like a good idea at the time."

Landfill turned away, face buried in her hands. Sank to the floor, mercifully next to and not IN her own puke-puddle.

"Jesus, Jimmy," Landfill mumbled through her hands. "What do you mean?"

Santa-Jimmy felt all the Christmas confidence that'd imbued him since his out-of-body experience seep out of his shoes. His shoulders slumped, and a little voice inside his head that sounded less like St. Nick and more like the middle-aged, diabetic, bad-backed warehouse manager he actually was said, *happy now, genius?*

"I, uh," Santa-Jimmy managed, trying to look at anything that wasn't the girl or Zombie-Tommy, "figured we needed a hand."

"Yeah, so you reanimated my boyfriend?"

"Not exactly. He was lying there, I just—I'm still his boss, okay? He didn't quit, he died. So, I snapped my fingers, he came running. Walking."

"What the fuck, how can you say that!"

"I'm sorry, okay?"

Landfill looked up at him, eyes red and watery, but not exactly crying. "This is hard enough to deal with without you, you, PARADING him around in front of me!"

Zombie-Tommy must've finally grokked they were talking about him, because he moaned something noncommittal about brains and shuffled over to the corner.

"Look, LINNEA," Santa-Jimmy emphasized her birth name, because he felt like Santa shouldn't be calling somebody Landfill, even if she asked, "you think I like this? I'm going to jot my own name down on my naughty list. Hell, we get through this, you can read me the riot act, kick me in the dick, whatever you want."

Landfill scoffed. "What was he doing in the basement, anyway? How'd the trucker get him all the way down there?"

Santa-Jimmy looked down at his feet. "I maybe didn't explain everything right." And then it all tumbled out, the real story. What happened. What HE did. Landfill's face grew red, she looked like she was about to snap, smash him over the head with her hammer. But she looked away, and when Santa-Jimmy finally finished hemming and hawing she was silent for a long moment.

Then—"I can't believe he just wanted to give me a

present." She turned to address the zombie in the corner. "Tommy? You know I wouldn't have cared, right? All I ever wanted for Christmas—"

"Wasssss youuuuu," Zombie-Tommy said, turning and clasping both hands over his heart.

Landfill let out one last sob, then turned back to Santa-Jimmy, resolute. "Screw it, this is all the elf's fault and we're going to have to work together. If we do this, can you bring him back? Like, all the way back?"

Santa-Jimmy mustered up his best rosy-cheeked grin, even if it did feel a little lopsided under the circumstances. "I was gonna try to do that anyway, but yeah. I'll see what I can do, okay?"

She swallowed hard, then nodded. "Let's go."

They brought the reindeer up first, forming a human chain with Zombie-Tommy at the bottom, Santa-Jimmy in the middle, and normal-Landfill passing decorations through the hatch.

But then they had the problem of the sleigh.

"You sure you have to take off from the roof?" Landfill asked.

"Yep. All the songs, Santa's always landing on a roof, taking off from a roof. Don't want to mess around."

"Huh." Landfill regarded the opening in the roof. "Have you measured?"

Santa-Jimmy shook his head. "What's the point? No way that's going—"

"Wait," Landfill said. "I have an idea. How about a Christmas miracle?"

"That was just counteracting some elf-venom. This? This is changing the laws of physics."

Landfill pointed at Zombie-Tommy. "And the theory of relativity allows for THAT?"

Zombie-Tommy looked down at his boots.

"That was management, not magic," Santa-Jimmy said. "But point taken. Look, I don't know how this stuff works. What if you only get one miracle each, and you use it up on this instead of—" He gestured at Zombie-Tommy, "You know."

Landfill's face screwed up in determination. "If you don't stop that bomb, none of it'll matter anyway."

"Yeah, okay. Let's give it a go. You got a present?"

"No. Unless—" Landfill rustled through the compartment in the back of the plastic sleigh, emerged a second later with a gift the size of a shoebox. "Whoa!"

"Guess we got lucky. Okay, okay, you been a good little girl this year? What do you want more than anything in the world?"

"To get this—" Landfill's voice broke, just for a moment, "—sleigh up to the roof."

Santa-Jimmy pointed at the present. "Do your thing."

Landfill tore through the wrapping paper, opening the box. Her face went wide with surprise. She reached in, tentatively.

Pulled out the biggest fucking dildo Santa-Jimmy had ever seen.

"Ew."

"Ew indeed," Santa-Jimmy said.

Landfill tossed both dildo and packaging aside and grabbed the other end of the sleigh. "Let's see if it worked."

Together they hefted it up the ladder, grunting and groaning, and when they reached the top?

Miracle of miracles!

It did.

```
11:53pm Pacific Standard Time
```

The basement lights clicked on. A silhouette appeared at the top of the stairs, looking like an oversized bowling pin with arms and legs.

The Mall Santa descended the steps one at a time.

Inside, Elfphonso felt himself losing control. Humans weren't meant to be piloted like the giant robots they sometimes requested for Christmas, and his tendrils were losing their grip on the man's neurons.

No matter. His goal was in sight.

Beyond the cluttered basement, the storage room door yawned open, darkness beyond. And beyond that, his brethren, his lieutenants. The means with which he'd overrun the globe. Topple the Clausian Hegemony and slaughter every single last one of those—

The Mall Santa tripped over an anthropomorphic toothbrush holding a shepherd's crook.

Which was also a toothbrush.

"Oof!" Elfphonso said, because he was also jacked into the man's pain receptors, which seemed like a good idea at the time until he banged his forehead against a metal shelf. Blood ran from his scalp, obscuring the vision of both elf and man.

Elfphonso wiped the Mall Santa's face clean with the back of his red-furred sleeve, struggled to his feet. He stumbled across the basement, more careful now, and reached the small room where he'd been unceremoniously birthed back into the world. Previously, the room had been redolent with pine and peppermint, but now it mostly smelled like shit and other assorted bodily fluids, most of which were smeared on the concrete.

But who cared about that, when the best Christmas present a murderous elf-zombie could ever imagine lay within?

ULTIMATE POWER.

Elfphonso carefully—reverently—pulled a snow globe from the crate. The interior was obscured by swirling flakes. But that didn't matter.

He knew what was inside, and how to open it.

He spun and smashed the snow globe on the ground, coughing as a thick gas spewed into the air. Waving it away, Elfphonso blinked the Mall Santa's eyes and said, "Brother? It is I, Elfphonso!"

No response.

Elfphonso frowned, eyebrows tickling the insides of the Mall Santa's digestive tract. "Huh. Maybe they mixed some regular snow globes in. I'll try another—"

As he reached into the crate, a long shadow suddenly fell over him. He turned, fists bunching, jaws snapping open.

Sergeant Matt Kringle, late of the Krampus Corps, stood in the doorway, covered in blood and pus and ew-the-fuck-is-that. "I bet you thought I was dead."

He took a step into the room, gore-mottled combat knife low at his side.

Elfphonso backpedaled, bumping into the crate. "I mean, I did . . . "

"Lollipopland couldn't kill me," Kringle snarled, lunging forward. "You never stood a Frostyman's chance in July."

Elfphonso wanted to point out a Frostyman could do quite well in certain parts of the Southern Hemisphere in that particular month, but he was too busy screaming and trying to claw his way out the back of the Mall Santa, but the stupid spine was in the way, and pretty soon Kringle finished his impromptu C-section (the C standing for Christmas, natch) and ripped the elf, screaming, back into the world.

"Shit."

11:57pm Pacific Standard Time

High above the Whosgotta Christmas Supply Warehouse, twin stars rocketed out of their respective yonders, arcing across the sky in a veiled threat to converge just over the heads of Santa-Jimmy, Landfill, and Zombie-Tommy.

The night had grown colder, but it didn't bother Santa-Jimmy one bit. Between beard and belly and general Santahood he seemed pretty well insulated from the weather.

Extra weird, because the assless leather chaps that came with the bizarre bondage sleigh were definitely designed to let in a draft.

"You sure this is gonna work?" Landfill asked.

Santa-Jimmy looked at the plastic sleigh. The gimp reindeer. Screwdolph's dick-nose. He shrugged. "If it does, it's gonna be the strangest Christmas miracle this town has ever seen. Here goes nothing."

He held up his palms in the direction of the plastic sleigh and the nine gimp-suited reindeer. He sucked in a breath, threw his head back and yelled, "Reindeer! I am your master! Come alive, come alive!" He waved his hands around.

Nothing happened.

Santa-Jimmy frowned, lay hands on either side of Screwdolph's head like a Pentecostal preacher, and repeated the same mantra.

Nothing.

The hatch banged open. Santa-Jimmy whirled, crowbar in his hands, prepared to bash some zombie brains, while Landfill brandished her hammer.

Sergeant Matt Kringle stepped onto the roof, holding Elfphonso by the neck. The elf hung limply, his arms and legs broken like an abused marionette.

Zombie-Tommy hissed at the elf.

Kringle shot a glance at the sky. "No time. We need liftoff, right now."

"And then when I get up there, I—"

Kringle waved dismissively. "You'll do what you do. Now hurry, make with the Christmas magic."

"It's not working."

"What do you mean?"

"He's trying," Landfill said. "Nothing's happening."

"Who cares," Elfphonso mumbled. "Christmas is ruined anyway."

Kringle bopped him on top of the head, then pointed at Santa-Jimmy. "Get in the sleigh."

Santa-Jimmy shrugged and sat on the plastic bench, expecting it to collapse under his weight.

But it didn't.

"Take up the reins," Kringle ordered.

Santa-Jimmy grabbed the reins—fine faux-silver chains.

"Now, call them by their names."

"Do what now?"

Kringle patted a reindeer on the head with his free hand. "In the songs. On Dasher, on Donner?"

Santa-Jimmy nodded animatedly. Finally, somebody was speaking his language.

"It's on *Dancer,*" Landfill said. "Y'know—" She broke into song.

"On Dasher, on Dancer, on Prancer and Vixen
On Comet, on Cupid, on Donner and Blitzen!"

"Oh yeah," Santa-Jimmy said, and started singing along, eyeing the reindeer, hoping they'd blink their way to life, ferry him off into the sky.

Still nothing.

Above, the twin shooting stars grew ever closer, to each other and Pine Canyon.

"Wait," Landfill said, shushing Jimmy, "what if those aren't their names?"

"Huh?"

Landfill leaned down to check out one of the gimpy reindeer. Just under the ball gag, there was a leather collar.

With a bright silver name tag.

"This is Daddy," Landfill said brightly, nearly

skipping over to the next. "And Sissy. And—" She quickly rattled off the rest of the reindeer, each name filthier and more ridiculous than the last.

"Call out their names!" Kringle said. Elfphonso squirmed half-boneless in his grasp. Kringle held him out over the warehouse roof, gave him a shake.

Elfphonso got the message.

Santa-Jimmy slapped the reins, steeled his nerves, and tried not to giggle as he sang—

"On Mistress, on Master, on Countess and Queen!
On Daddy, on Cockslut, on Sissy, and Peen!
Oh yeah—and ON SCREWDOLPH!"

The nine gimpy reindeer sprang to sexy life, hooves tap-tap-tapping on the rooftop, neighing and braying and begging someone to please, please hurt them good.

Santa-Jimmy yelled "Ho, ho, ho, let's go!"

Yanked back the reins.

And, one by one, those nine gimpy reindeer raced across the rooftop, faster and faster, until their hooves were skimming air, and then they were off, zooming across the sky, towards those two colliding stars.

11:59pm Pacific Standard Time

Landfill stood on the roof, watching the sleigh hurtle upwards. The two missiles were perilously close now. She couldn't believe it. She never thought she'd die in a nuclear explosion, and definitely not on CHRISTMAS. Nothing about it seemed fair.

"Hurrrgh," a voice softly said at her shoulder, then a cold, clammy palm slipped into her own.

She looked to her right, and there was Zombie-Tommy, squeezing her hand, doing this weird half-smile thing with his half-face, and it was kind of sickening but kind of charming, and she thought to herself, well, at least we'll get to go out together.

"I love you," Zombie-Tommy gurgled. "And brains. But mostly you."

Landfill's heart grew three sizes, she squealed and leaned into him, most of the smell thankfully whipped away by the wind. "I love you too, you big goof."

Kringle joined them, looking up at the sky. Even Elfphonso tracked the sleigh's progress.

"Clauses are such assholes," he said.

"One thing we can agree on, little guy," Kringle said, lightly patting his head.

They stood like that for a long moment, former Krampus Corps sergeant, crippled elf, Christpunk and Juggalo, and maybe there's some kind of message about the true meaning of Christmas in there, or maybe it was just a really fucked up tableau of broken people who'd gotten fucked by the granddaddy of all holidays and the scheming, power-mad assholes behind the curtain.

The sleigh was just a dot, barely discernible against the night sky.

And then that dot collided with the twin shooting stars, and everything went white.

December 25th, 2019
12:00am Pacific Standard Time
CHRISTMAS GODDAMN DAY

Landfill blinked, an act that surprised the hell out of her, because she thought for sure that white flash was everybody dying. Later she'd wonder how the hell she wasn't blinded, and chalk it up to yet another Christmas miracle or maybe just super lazy writing, who the fuck knows?

The shooting stars were gone. In their place, Santa-Jimmy's face stretched across the sky, made of burning points of light. He grinned, and his booming voice shook the night, setting off car alarms as far away as Las Vegas.

"Ho, ho, ho! Merry Christmas to all—Christpunks, Jugglers, that Army guy what's his name—"

"Kringle," Matt Kringle muttered.

"And screw it, the elf too. He might be a little shit, but way I heard it, that's more on the Clauses than anything, making him the way he is."

"Damn right," Elfphonso squeaked.

"Remember the true meaning of Christmas, and Hannukah, and Kwanzaa, and don't forget Cesar Chavez day. Earth Day, that's a good one. Thanksgiving, hell, I call that baby Christmas. And Halloween. If a Halloween supply warehouse were economically viable, maybe I woulda worked there, and none of this would have ever happened."

"Kind of a long speech for a guy made of

fireworks," Elfphonso muttered, and the three others—even Zombie-Tommy—shushed him.

"But it did, and I died absorbing a nuclear explosion, but don't be sad. I'm the goddamn Spirit of Christmas, so I'm not really dead, it's actually kind of a *Star Wars* thing, which I'm now qualified to say IS a Christmas movie, but—I digress."

And then he exclaimed, as he blinked out of sight, "Merry Christmas to all—"

"And to all a good night," Landfill screamed back.

Then his visage faded from the sky, and all was finally silent.

"Oh yeah," Santa-Jimmy said, blazing back into existence. "One last thing. You know that Christmas miracle you wanted, Linnea? For a minute there I became one with the cosmos and turns out I can kinda pull it off."

Zombie-Tommy's hand grew warm in hers and Landfill gasped.

"Only problem is, I only know what he looks like with makeup on, so that's basically his skin now, but somehow I don't think that'll be a problem."

Landfill turned, and Tommy, HER Tommy, was smiling down at her through all that greasepaint.

"Whoop whoop, baby," Tommy said with a grin. "Juggalos for life."

"Literally," Santa-Jimmy boomed. "Okay, smell you later." He let out one final ho-ho-ho and faded, for the final time, out of sight.

"I thought you were dead," Landfill said, cupping Tommy's face in hers. "I thought I lost you!"

"Wasn't gonna leave my baby alone on Christmas," Tommy said, and kissed her with such fiery passion all the mistletoe in the warehouse below shriveled up and died, then leaned down and whispered in her ear, "Also?

"I TOTALLY got you a present."

12:29am Pacific Standard Time

Sergeant Matt Kringle hauled himself into the big rig and sat, eyeing the controls. Stars twinkled through the dusty windshield. He'd piloted all manner of sleighs but had to think back to basic training to remember how to handle one of the odd, earthbound, dinosaur-juice-fueled human vehicles.

"You sure I can take this?" he asked.

Landfill and Tommy stood just outside the door, arm-in-arm, smiling up at him.

"Sure thing," Landfill said. "I kinda killed the guy it belonged to, so really you're helping us get rid of evidence."

"Well then," Kringle said, and gave the horn a test honk.

Loud. He liked that.

"Let's get this show on the road!" shouted Elfphonso from the passenger seat, where they'd turned a little plastic manger into a carrying tote for him. "Next stop, North Pole."

"In about two weeks," Kringle said. "But yeah, we'll get there."

"Are you sure you wanna be traveling with that, that, thing?" Tommy asked.

Kringle looked at the brutalized elf monster in the plastic bassinet. "Jimmy was right. The Clauses made him what he is. I'm going to go back to the Pole, put my goddamn boot up all their asses, and see if their scientists can turn him back to normal."

"Or a minotaur!" Elfphonso shrieked. "That'd be bitchin!"

"Please don't turn him into a minotaur," Landfill said.

Kringle smiled tightly. "Don't worry. The Clausian Hegemony's done conducting unethical experiments. AND invading Lollipopland."

"Lollipopland?" Tommy asked.

"Long story, kid." Kringle fired up the engine and dropped it into gear. "Merry Christmas, the both of you."

"Merry Christmas to you too!"

Kringle nodded and took off, turning the big rig in one long, lazy circle, before cruising out of the Whosgotta Christmas Supply Warehouse parking lot. The whole time, he kept one eye on the side view mirror, watching the two young lovers at the loading dock, each waving animatedly.

"Haven't had a friend in years," Kringle said quietly to himself.

He turned onto the road, reflecting on all he'd experienced, all he'd seen. Part of him was weary.

But another part? The best part?

Knew the battle was just beginning.

"If you put me on the dash, we can play I Spy!" Elfphonso said.

"Fine," Kringle said, steering with his knees. Taking his eyes off the road just long enough to give his new friend a hand.

`12:37am Pacific Standard Time`

Caterpillar groaned and rolled over. His head hurt. His neck hurt. So did his legs, which he figured was a pretty good thing, pain and movement going hand-in-hand like they did. He rubbed his face and opened his eyes.

Found himself lying in a ditch.

Self-Harm's golf cart was a few feet away, upside-down with the roof caved in. The skid marks on the asphalt told the rest of the story. His memory was fuzzy, but Caterpillar didn't need to remember what happened to know he was well and truly fucked.

He'd stolen Self-Harm's golf cart, his friend's prized possession. And not just stolen, TOTALED. Self-Harm was probably sitting on the side of the road somewhere, angrily singing carols to himself and plotting a really fucked up revenge.

Caterpillar rubbed his head, looked at his fingers. A little dried blood, but nothing fresh. He'd gotten off easy.

Physically, at least.

He stood up—legs shaky but holding—and climbed out of the ditch. Reaching the road, he suddenly noticed all the flakes in the air.

Caterpillar goggled at the sight—snow, here? In Southern California?

It was a Christmas miracle!

The crashed golf cart temporarily forgotten,

RETURN OF THE LIVING ELVES

Caterpillar threw back his head, stuck out his tongue, and pirouetted in wide, lazy circles, too concussed to realize the "snowflakes" landing on his tongue were actually a mixture of asbestos and fricasseed zombie from several of the structure fires still burning across the greater Pine Canyon metropolitan area.

Nor did he notice the big rig barreling down on him.

Caterpillar danced, the truck squealed across the pavement, and then, just when it seemed like all was lost, one last Christmas miracle happened!

Just kidding, that motherfucker got WRECKED.

Merry Christmas, bitches.

THE MURDEROUS EEJIT

SHELLY LYONS

I SMELLED HER FIRST. Vanilla cake with a thin layer of jam. Then Eliza herself strolled by, alone in the small hours wearing her club clothes. Clearly out trolling for bad decisions, like the eejit she was. Booksmart, no doubt about it, but when it came to men, the girl was always anglin' for her next mistake.

Admittedly, I was one of those mistakes, though I'll wager I was her best.

If you asked, 'Was it your giant Irish wang giving her the good business?' I might tell you about those times we drank tequila and she'd scream, "Fuck me blind!" and God love her, I tried, giving her such a go 'til she became Helen Keller and I, the amoral winds of fate.

But the new, truth-telling Clarky should add that during my year in a manky Belfast jail, wherein I saw more sausage in the communal shower than ever in the school showers, I got to realizing mine was on the wee side. Ergo, someone had lied to me long ago.

Being an industrious young lad, I spent the year between jail and moving to America perfecting the art of cunnilingus like a musician mastering his instrument, until I could truthfully crown myself king of the clamshell and tweak the lovelies into a fever pitch. Once accomplished, Fun Sacks and Bitsy Boy joined the party, happy as a bunch o' Catholics the Saturday before confession.

This was the Clarky who drove Eliza wild with a bit of wang and lick.

"Hello, luv," I said as she passed me, with not a flick of an eye my way.

Me, now a ghost, cursed to ever-loiter in the alleyway where I took a final knife plunge to the gut, still yearned for any type of contact with the ladies, especially one of those who always took my after-midnight calls.

She turned the corner. But I couldn't let her go. "Float, Clarky," I said, and hovered above the pavement. This was as much as I believed I could do. But tonight I added, "Follow, Clarky," and Lord love me, off I trailed behind her! Flummoxed by this new ability, I followed her all the way home, whilst mourning the many lost nights of babes gone by and myself unaware I could simply ghost-stalk them home to watch them take baths.

But God as my witness, my sincere aim in tagging along with Eliza was to be her shepherd, repay a bit of the kindness she showed me whenever I fancied a squeeze.

After we entered her apartment, my fingers greedily plunged into her head full o' curls, but just passed on through per usual, the bloody useless spectral twats.

"Luv, luv, give us a kiss!" I shouted, unheard. Oh,

to see that shy lopsided grin portending a future of nasty mashing, or a faint twitch of her bewitching eyes. But who was I joshing? Not even my own true God was touchable, the poor bastard hanging idle as a sleeping worm.

Still, finally freed of the alley, I decided to hang around a bit. Her pad became my haunting grounds, yet I could not haunt. How did other ghosts interact with the living? If someone had to guess what old Clarky'd do in ghost form, it would be "no good,' 'heavy mischief,' 'ghost-fucking the ladies,' and all that. But I merely sat on her couch, though I felt no velour cushions on my bottom, or floated above her bed, though incapable of plummeting atop her.

My world became one of surveillance: Eliza eating, bathing, sleeping, crying, arguing with her ma on the phone, or staring at the TV whilst filing her toenails. Oh, what I'd give to suck on those toes.

The air got cold, and Eliza went out to buy a Christmas tree, then came home and decorated it alone, humming carols and doing a bit o' boo-hooing over family photos. In this moment, my heart grew soft and mucky in a way I'd never felt before.

After that, I continued following her to clubs, but now, seeing her bang strangers in the handicap stalls was giving me the weeps. Aye, weepy I'd become. All those years I called when drunk, plundered her goodies, then sailed off to lusher shores; all those times I told her she was no Bridget Bardot but that she still made me hard—and then didn't understand why that hurt her—I was done with all that, spectral hand pressed over ghost heart. Now, I loved her. God help me, I loved her.

A few nights before Christmas, I, being in no mood to observe her slutty shenanigans, skipped shadowing her to a club, and spent the evening dandering about the neighborhood 'til she returned. I soared through treetops past the holiday lights and Santa displays, peeked in neighbors' windows in hopes of finding real-life pornography, but getting an eyeful of nothing but couch taters staring blank-faced at their tellies or families decorating trees. I was going outta of my phantom skull with boredom, when one of them ride share cars with the lights in the window dropped Eliza off in front of the apartment.

The car flicked off its lights and parked. Inside, a pugilist type with a smashy nose and Neanderthal eyebrows pulled out his Johnny Pee and wanked it as he watched my luv walk inside.

Unlike mortal Clarky who'd target the biggest lad in a group to head-butt, dead me had no power to stop him. I banged on the windshield, but no cracks were made. I barked into his ear like a mad dog, but he did not flinch. Oh, curse my vaporous fists! Curse my mute threats!

The grunting animal yanked it, but like my own it stayed fudgy. My excuse was being deceased. Here, weeping, growling and pounding the dashboard was a deranged feck lacking the essential umph to gas up the jeeter. His sniffles petered until he quieted. Then he turned off the idling car. I, being two inches from his oily eyes, saw intent reflecting back in the form of Eliza tottering in heels to her door.

Despite his bulk, this pig face in a leather bomber jacket oozed out of the car like a phantom, and lurked in the shadows where the street lights didn't spill. He hyperventilated, ape-pounded his chest. A familiar trick. It's how I always found a fight, stole a motorcycle, chased the best looking woman who'd never look at me twice in the light of day. He was summoning his inner animal, and it looked mean.

If only I could touch something! Rage grew until I could feel the old plunge and twist of the knife in my gut.

"Quit your gurning, Clarky," I told myself. "You got the floating and the following down, all by thinking about it." So, I pictured what to do next, and shot up into the sky, past street lights, through clouds, into the dark of space. Brilliant! Then, remembering my mission, I turned myself around, yelled towards earth: "You will feel my wrath!" and nosedived, aiming for the animal stalking across her lawn.

Had I been muscle and bone, that fecking eejit would've obliterated into a puddle on the walkway, but the impact of ghost Clarky felt like a drop of water cresting over a mushroom.

Yet, a dainty gasp was heard! And beefy hands swept across his chrome dome. I'd done this! I'd done something!

Still, his eyes flicked over to the window, to that screen I knew needed a fix—the edge of it being twisted outwards from the time Eliza lost her key and had to break in. I'd wanted to open the door for her, I did. Sometimes a ghost man feels so useless he'd like to kill himself, but can't, Lord help his eejit soul, he can't.

A meaty finger poked at the screen's frame. Hesitant, as though still working up to the idea. He gulped some foggy night air and turned to the front door, politely tapping on it with hairy knuckles.

Soon enough, our eejit girl opened the door a crack, she being still so pink-cheeked and pretty after the alcohol and second-hand smoke. "Hi, oh, hi . . . " she widened the door to shoe-width.

"I think you left your phone in the car," he said in a voice I wouldn't expect him to possess, so smooth and unthreatening it rang.

"Oh, what?" She glanced behind her for a split second. "No, I'm looking at it—"

He flat-handed the door open and it banged against her head, sending her off her shoes as he bounded inside, stifling her outcry with a slabby hand.

What's a man made o' mere vapor supposed to do? Was this penance for a life spent indulging all my wanton impulses? To behold the one girl truly kind to me getting shoved onto the couch? To hear her head conk against the remote control, turning on the TV? If this be penance, then I prefer the brimstone, thank you.

The big man grabbed the remote, turning up its volume on the old black and white movie enough to drown out her squealing but not so loud as to alert the neighbors.

"What is it you want, Mary? What do you want? You want the moon? Just say the word . . . "

If I'd been able to zoom up into space and dive bomb the beast, it followed that I might whip around the living room like when Superman flew around earth to reverse time. I'd keep my Lois Lane from being sullied by this goblin if I had to forever whirl in a frenzied ellipsis.

As before, I envisioned then manifested the

action, traveling every corner, over and under furniture, in and out of walls. Moving so fast everything blurred. Yet from the corners of my eyes, I saw the great beast tear off her blouse.

"No!" My journey evolved into a tornado, it did. There'd be no stopping until I could push into the world around me. How would this end? In life it always ended with a Resisting arrest charge. In death? I had no idea.

"Eliza! Eliza! Eliza!" I bellowed. "You're better than Bridget Bardot, luv! She got to be an old racist and you're still young enough to bitch-hooks a fellow!"

The fiend hoisted his bulk atop my girl, whose wails barely escaped through the space between his cruddy fingers.

"I luv ye, Eliza! I luv ye!" I cried as he seized her throat.

The heat of flame burned around me. Lights strobed in my periphery. The Christmas tree wobbled! One of the glittery balls fell off the tree, then another! My talents had grown, they had! Now, squinting through my blindness, I saw the monster's head crane around as though he felt the power of Clarky upon him, and that is when I flew at him with the goal of maximum destruction.

If the first impact had been a raindrop, this jobby was a right splash of the hose. His hands raked across his naked dome, which gave my girl an opening. Sure enough, her arm emerged from his bulk, scrabbling across the table till she found her nail file and jabbed it into his arm with a banshee's shriek.

He roared and backhanded her across the face

before toppling off the couch, thus fully unpinning my girl, who wasted no time setting upon him, stabbing his cheek and his temple, then honing in on the eye. "Call the police!" she screamed for the neighbors to hear. She extracted the file from his eye socket, pulling out a hefty dollop of goop as her attacker howled.

His fat hands cupped the gaping eyehole as she chicken-stomped his chest, followed by a stabby-stabby in the neck and a glorious gushing red fountain. His body flopped about, then grew still. A puff of red smoke emerged from his sternum and began to take his shape.

"Oh, it's a brawl you want, fat boy?" I cocked my fists and forehead, ready to rumble. But, before he materialized in full, the eejit shrank back to mist and wafted away through the wall. "Coward!"

Ach! Here I was feeling deprived of a ghost brawl, when my girl began shivering, rocking herself back and forth as the sirens drew close and the pretty girl on TV said, *"George Bailey, give me back my robe!"*

My hand stroked Eliza's blood-soaked cheek, wishing she knew how I'd helped. Or that I could wish her a merry Christmas, buy her a gift, put a cookie out for Santa, put a wee Clarky cookie up her Wookiee, or get a response to my touch. Ach, these rewards were too lofty for a single good deed. But, oh what I'd give for one of her lopsided grins . . .

What's this now? My wee lad was stiffening!

Glory be, I thought, reaching for him, then stopped myself.

"Hello, old mate, let's do this some other time."

Instead, I blew into Eliza's ear. She always liked that.

ABOUT THIS DUDE

Brian Asman is a writer, editor, producer and actor from San Diego, CA. He's the author of *I'm Not Even Supposed to Be Here Today* from Eraserhead Press and *Labor Day, Man, Fuck This House, Nunchuck City* and *Jailbroke* from Mutated Media. He's recently published short stories in the anthologies *Breaking Bizarro, Welcome to the Splatter Club* and *Lost Films*, and comics in *Tales of Horrorgasm*. An anthology he co-edited with Danger Slater, *Boinking Bizarro*, was recently released by Death's Head Press. He holds an MFA from UCR-Palm Desert. He's represented by Dunham Literary, Inc. Max Booth III is his hype man. Find him on social media as @thebrianasman or his website www.brianasmanbooks.com.

Here's a picture he drew of a bad Santa:

ABOUT THIS LADY

This Hollywood townie wrote a bunch of marketing verbiage and screenplays before reinventing herself as a narrative prose writer. Her horror/sci-fi novel, *Like Real*, will enter the world via PGhoulish Books in 2023. She would be delighted to discuss made-for-television horror films and thrillers with you.

CPSIA information can be obtained
at www.ICGtesting.com
Printed in the USA
JSHW021239111122
33016JS00003B/8